PUFFIN BOOKS

# Wilma's Wicked Revenge

Kaye Umansky was born in Plymouth, Devon. Her favourite books as a child were the *Just William* books, *Alice's Adventures in Wonderland*, *The Hobbit* and *The Swish of the Curtain*. She went to teachers' training college, and then she taught in London primary schools for twelve years, specializing in music and drama. In her spare time she sang and played keyboards with a semi-professional soul band.

She now writes full-time – or as full-time as she can in between trips to Sainsbury's and looking after her husband (Mo), daughter (Ella, aged thirteen) and cats (Charlie and Alfie).

*Some other books by Kaye Umansky*

PONGWIFFY
PONGWIFFY AND THE GOBLINS' REVENGE
PONGWIFFY AND THE SPELL OF THE YEAR
PONGWIFFY AND THE HOLIDAY OF DOOM
PONGWIFFY AND THE PANTOMIME

THE FWOG PWINCE: THE TWUTH!

*Non-fiction*

DO NOT OPEN BEFORE CHRISTMAS DAY!

*For Younger Readers*

THE JEALOUS GIANT
THE ROMANTIC GIANT
TICKLE MY NOSE AND OTHER STORIES

Kaye Umansky

# Wilma's Wicked Revenge

*Illustrated by Tony Blundell*

PUFFIN BOOKS

PUFFIN BOOKS

Published by the Penguin Group
Penguin Books Ltd, 27 Wrights Lane, London W8 5TZ, England
Penguin Putnam Inc., 375 Hudson Street, New York, New York 10014, USA
Penguin Books Australia Ltd, Ringwood, Victoria, Australia
Penguin Books Canada Ltd, 10 Alcorn Avenue, Toronto, Ontario, Canada M4V 3B2
Penguin Books (NZ) Ltd, Private Bag 102902, NSMC, Auckland, New Zealand

On the World Wide Web at: www.penguin.com

Penguin Books Ltd, Registered Offices: Harmondsworth, Middlesex, England

First published 2000
1 3 5 7 9 10 8 6 4 2



Set in Bembo

Made and printed in England by Clays Ltd, St Ives plc



British Library Cataloguing in Publication Data
A CIP catalogue record for this book is available from the British Library

ISBN 0–141–30442–1



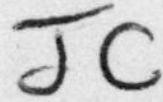

# CONTENTS

# 1. MY BIRTHDAY TEA

So. There I was on the night of my twelfth birthday, propped up in bed, stuffing my face with cake and attempting to play the blues on my new mouth organ.

Birthday cake in bed is *not* a good idea. There were crumbs in the sheets and great dollops of butter-icing all over the pillow. My teeth were stuck up with marzipan. I had made big inroads into the cake, but there was still a long way to go. Determinedly, I picked up another chunk and, feeling rather sick, crammed it down.

Now, you're probably thinking that's a weird thing to be doing on your birthday. Sitting in bed forcing cake down your throat all on your own.

But then, *you* probably have a normal family.

Mother had organized a nice tea, I'll give her that.

Sausage rolls and chocolate biscuits and little cakes and jellies. Of course, she hadn't prepared any of this *herself*. She's the Queen of the Night. It's a demanding job involving antisocial hours and she doesn't have time for such things. She'd just given a list to Mrs Pudding, our cook, and left her to get on with it.

There were five of us seated at the long table in the Great Hall: Mother, Daddy, Grandma, Uncle Bacchus and me. We sat in doleful silence, eyeing the feast before us and not touching a crumb. I wasn't even allowed to open my presents. Nothing could begin, you see, until *they* turned up. I am referring to Frostia and Scarlettine. My rotten sisters. One is Queen of the Snow and one is Queen of Mirrors. They're older than me. They have proper titles and their own castles. Apparently, that gives them the right to not send a card and to turn up late to people's birthday teas.

We had been waiting for an hour. It had been a very *long* hour. Grandma was asleep. Just as well, really. She's not much fun when she's awake. At one point, Daddy tried to brighten things up by tinkling out a jolly little rhythm on his glass with a fork, but Mother quelled him with a Look and he resorted to building a little pyramid with sugar cubes.

Uncle Bacchus kept taking surreptitious little nips from the secret flask he carries inside his toga. Once, his hand crept towards a plateful of crisps, but Mother rapped him on the knuckles with her fan. She was growing anxious, I could tell. Her Aura was getting darker. (That's the patch of darkness that always surrounds her. It comes with the job.)

There was a discreet cough from the kitchen doorway and Peevish the butler came creaking in.

"Excuse me, ma'am," he murmured, knee joints cracking as he genuflected before Mother. "Mrs Pudding begs to inquire whether you're ready for the cake yet?"

"Yes," I said.

"No," said Mother. "Ask her to give it another few minutes, would you?"

"It's her Bingo night, ma'am," warned Peevish. "She's already got her coat on."

"Oh dear. George, what shall we do? I don't want to start without the girls, but I daren't upset Mrs Pudding . . ."

"*Hark!*" We all jumped, apart from Grandma. Uncle Bacchus was holding up a finger for silence. "I hear hoofs! And sleigh bells, unless I'm very much mistaken!"

Relief washed over the table like a tidal wave.

"It's them!" trilled Mother. "They've arrived!"

They certainly know how to make an entrance, my sisters. The doors crashed open to the sound of a fanfare provided by guards in scarlet livery. We don't bother with guards in the Ancestral Halls on informal family occasions, so they'd brought their own. Typical.

Scarlettine was all in red, as usual. She had Kissy-Woo in her arms. Kissy-Woo is her dog – a pampered, fat little fiend sporting a red ribbon tied around its daft top-knot. Behind Scarlettine loomed Frostia – all six feet of her. She was dressed from head to foot in white. Cold white face, white hair, white fur cloak and a tall crown made of ice.

"Welcome, darlings!" cried Mother.

"*Mother!*" cooed Scarlettine, dropping her cloak on the floor for Peevish to pick up.

"Hello, everyone," drawled Frostia, advancing into the Hall. The temperature immediately dropped by several degrees. "It's very warm in here. Do you mind?"

She pointed a white finger at the blazing fire at the far end of the Hall. Instantly, it went out.

"Good evening, Miss Frostia, your most royal and *exquisitely* chilly majesty," oiled Peevish. "May I say how lovely you are looking."

"*Ooh!*" cried Scarlettine, putting on a baby pout. "What about me then, Peevish? Don't *I* look lovely?"

"That goes without saying, Miss Scarlettine," slimed Peevish, the silly old git. "No one is lovelier than you. In fact, if I might be so bold, you are indeed the fairest of them all."

"And don't you forget it," said Scarlettine, mincing to the table, where I sat scowling in my old, brown, too-tight dress. "Is tea ready? I'm starving!"

"It's been ready for the last hour," I snarled.

"*Ooh!* Get *you*! You're so *uptight*, Wilma. You forget some of us have important things to do. We don't all lie around in bed all day stuffing our faces." She cast a meaningful look at my tummy and dropped into a chair. "*Ooh!* Chocolate cookies, Kissy-Woo! Your *favourite*!"

Peevish staggered off with the cloaks, leaving us on our own to make happy family-type conversation.

"Are we late or something?" inquired Frostia, peering down the frosty slope of her nose at the sandwiches, which were beginning to curl at the edges.

"Oh no, darling!" said Mother, giving me one of her Looks. "It's just that it's Mrs Pudding's night off and she's anxious to bring in the cake."

"I shouldn't have thought Wilma needed more cake," remarked Scarlettine spitefully, popping cookies into Kissy-Woo's gaping maw. "She's podgy enough already."

"*Must* she feed that dog at the table?" I said sourly. "Tell her, Mother."

"Take no notice of nasty Wilma," cooed Scarlettine, nuzzling the revolting mutt. "Kissy-Woo's family, aren't you, precious?"

I was about to remark that a hairball in a ribbon was no relation of mine, but just then the door to the kitchen opened. Mrs Pudding stood there in her firmly buttoned overcoat. One hand held her handbag. The other bore a plate containing a large, iced birthday cake with twelve candles twinkling on the top.

"So do you want this cake or don't you?" demanded Mrs Pudding.

"Oh yes!" cried Mother, clapping her hands. "Of course we do. How very, *very* kind of you to hang on, Mrs Pudding. And doesn't it look *lovely*, everyone?"

Murmurs of appreciation arose as Mrs Pudding stomped across and plonked the cake on the table.

"Right," she said sourly. "I'll be off."

"Oh, do stay and have a piece!" begged Mother. "She must, mustn't she, George?"

"No, thank you," sniffed Mrs Pudding, determined to punish us. "I'm already late as it is." And with that, she waddled out.

"Come on then, pet," said Daddy brightly. "Blow out the candles, eh? Then we can start the party."

Thrilled to be the centre of attention for a change, I took a deep breath. But before I could let it out, Frostia pointed a sly talon at the cake and all the candles went out! There was nothing left for me to blow.

Now, you might think that's a small thing to get upset about. But what you have to remember is, I've had to endure *years* of this sort of thing. It was just one more insult in a lifetime of petty meanness.

I stared down at my cake, a hundred little scenes replaying in flashback in my mind. Me in my pushchair, being tipped into the ornamental lake. Me being tied to a tree and left there all night, at the mercy of squirrels. Me being buried in the sandpit, me being locked out on the battlements in a blizzard, me bawling piteously over scribbled-on books and mangled toys while my sisters looked on, smirking. Can you blame me for overreacting? I think not.

"Did you *see* that?" I howled, outraged. "Did you *see* what she did?"

"I was getting too warm," explained Frostia, sounding pained. "All those candles. Why? Is there a problem?"

"*My* cake!" I shouted. "*My* candles! *My* birthday! Remember?"

"*Do* stop ranting, Wilma," sighed Mother. "The candles are out, and that's the end of it. Peevish will take the cake away and cut it up. Come on, everybody, party time! Tuck in!"

I could have gone on a hunger strike in protest, but I didn't want to cut my nose off to spite my face. So I ate. I ate a *lot*. In fact, I managed to put away three platefuls, while Mother and my two sisters nibbled on bits of cucumber and talked Queenly business in an undertone. It makes me furious the way they always leave me out. Just because I'm not a Queen yet.

When I'd eaten so much that I felt sick, I pulled a cracker with Daddy. Inside was a paper hat and a plastic ring. Neither fitted.

"Isn't that lovely?" said Daddy.

"No," I sulked.

"Dear me," he said. "My birthday girl doesn't sound very happy."

"I'm not," I said, glaring at Mother and my sisters, who had their heads together like three witches around a cauldron. "I never get any attention around here. Everyone makes a fuss of *them*. They're not *that* special."

"Of course not, of course not."

"I can be a Wicked Queen too. It's not that hard. I got better marks in my Grade Three Magic than *they* did."

"Still dabbling with Magic, are you? I don't know. You girls," said Daddy with a little sigh. He's never quite got the hang of this Wicked Queen business, despite being married to one. He's happiest pottering around the grounds of the Ancestral Halls trying to get tomatoes to ripen.

At that point, Uncle Bacchus offered him a swig from his secret flask and they started talking about gardening, so I didn't have anyone to moan at.

"Excuse *me*," I said sharply, when I could take no more. "Do you think I could open my presents perhaps? Seeing as it's my birthday?"

"Yes, of course, darling," said Mother vaguely. "As I was saying, Scarlettine . . ."

"Do *you* want to see me open my presents, Daddy?"

"Of course, pet, in a minute. So I tried putting lime down, but that didn't do any good. It's the lack of sun, you see . . ."

So I wandered over to the sideboard and opened my gifts. Of course, I didn't get anything I wanted, even though I had made a list. What I *wanted* was one of those new, expensive Crystal Balls with audio facilities. Plus a new wand, various Magical potions, a pony and trap, a decent watch, a puppy, a castle of my own, unlimited spending money and, above all, a title and a bit of respect around here.

What I *got* was a hairbrush from Mother, a wetting doll from Daddy (who still thinks I'm six), a Junior Knitting Kit from Grandma, a mouth organ from Uncle Bacchus, a bar of lemon soap from Mrs Pudding and a book from Peevish entitled *A Thousand Years of Cutlery*.

From Scarlettine? Nothing. From Frostia? Ditto.

"I think there's something missing here," I announced loudly.

"What's that, darling?" inquired Mother, adding, "Oh. You've opened your presents. Weren't they lovely? Aren't you a lucky girl?"

"I said there's something missing. Funnily enough, I don't see anything from Frostia or Scarlettine."

"I didn't have time," said Scarlettine immediately. "I've been *sooooo* busy, you wouldn't believe."

"I was going to stop off on the way, but all the shops were closed," said Frostia with a yawn.

"Never mind," said Mother. "What's important is, you've brought yourselves. Isn't that right, Wilma? Stop looking so *grim*, darling. Why don't you take your lovely new brush and go and do something about your hair?"

"I didn't want a new brush. It wasn't on my list, was it? I wanted a Crystal Ball with audio facilities . . ."

But she had turned away and was talking to Frostia.

"Now, darling. *Do* tell me all about your new extension. Have you had the frozen lake put in yet? I can't wait to come and see it . . ."

Speechless with disgust, I scooped up my pathetic gifts and stalked out of the Hall. Nobody even noticed. I went to my bedroom, making a detour to the kitchen to collect the birthday cake, which Peevish was cutting up.

"It's for everyone, Miss Wilma," he protested.

"It's for me," I told him. "My birthday. My cake. Give."

"Did you like the book?" he inquired. "It came free with the new spoons."

"Frankly, no," I said.

And I snatched the cake from him and stormed off to my bedroom.

## 2. CHUCKED OUT

And that's how I came to be in bed with my cake, trying to play the blues. The mouth organ didn't work very well. The fact that the holes were plugged up with cake didn't help. It finally clogged up altogether, so I threw it crossly on the floor and went to clean my teeth.

That depressed me even more, because I couldn't help catching a glimpse of my hair in the mirror.

My hair. My hair is so *unfair*. How come I'm the only female member of this family with horrible hair? I'm not counting Grandma, who goes in for the Wire Wool in Hairnet look. I'm talking about Mother and my sisters. You don't see Mother's often, because she usually wears a cowl. But when you do, it's a wonder to behold. Long, midnight black, with a silver streak. Frostia has this pure white mane which she piles on top of her head like a snow drift. Scarlettine has masses of shining red curls, which she tosses around a lot.

And mine? Four words. Mice tails in butter. Fill in the details yourself. I can't bear talking about it.

I glared at my hair, drank a glass of water, then scuttled back to bed, pausing only to brush a ton of cake crumbs on to the floor. I had just crawled back in and was about to blow out the candle when the door burst open.

"Out you get, *Wilma*!" announced Scarlettine, setting Kissy-Woo down. The vile little beast immediately made a puddle on my carpet. She was followed by Frostia, who immediately trod on my mouth organ with her high-heeled shoe. *Crunch*. That was that then.

"Get that dog out of here!" I howled.

"No," said Scarlettine, tugging at my blanket. "We're sleeping over."

"Not in here you're not," I said, hanging on like grim death. "There are a hundred rooms in this palace to choose from. Why pick mine?"

This is true. The Ancestral Halls ramble everywhere. No one even knows how far the dungeons go.

"Because it was ours first, wasn't it, Frosty?"

"Absolutely," agreed Frostia. You could tell she was in the room. The windows were beginning to ice over.

"Well, it's mine now," I said, still clinging to my blanket. "You've left home. Mother said I could have it."

"Tough. Tonight, we're back," spat Scarlettine, forcing my fingers open and yanking the blanket on to the floor. Frostia promptly stepped on it, so there was no chance of getting it back. Scarlettine gave a sharp laugh of triumph, then skipped over to the dressing table and began primping in the mirror.

"I'm telling Mother," I whined.

"You can't. She's off on The Round."

That's the trouble with having the Queen of the Night for a mother. She's never here at bedtime. She's off flying around the world, Bringing the Night, much too busy to deal with bad dreams or any childish little problems one might have. Come to think of it, she wouldn't be that interested anyway. She's a career woman. The Round comes first. It's no wonder I get resentful.

"You're such a *baby*, Wilma," sneered Frostia. "I dread to think what will happen when you're old enough to have a *title* and *a castle of your own*. Like Scarlettine and me."

*A title and a castle of your own*. It's a sore point and she knows it. They both have their own castles, as I've already mentioned. Frostia's is in the frozen north. I remember going to her house-chilling party. We all stood around while a load of creepy servants crept about the place armed with trays of frozen nibbly bits. Several of the guests went home with frostbite and Uncle Bacchus's knees were blue for weeks. There was an unpleasant incident involving wolves too. Frostia keeps wolves to pull her sleigh. They have names like Biter, Gnasher and Fango and are allowed to wander about the place taking chunks out of any guest they take a fancy to.

Scarlettine's castle, in contrast, is a hideous riot of red flock wallpaper and crimson carpets. There are mirrors on every wall because she can't go two minutes without looking at herself. She is, without doubt, the vainest creature ever born. I've never known anyone spend so much time primping and preening. Annoyingly, it seems to work. There is always a long queue of devoted suitors at her door, bearing armfuls of carnations and begging for her hand in marriage.

Of course, if they knew how dangerous she was, they'd run a mile. Scarlettine, you see, is an expert with poisons, as everyone found out to their cost the first time Mrs Pudding let her bake a cake, when she was about seven. Luckily, I was a baby at the time and still on mashed banana, so I missed out – but the incident has passed into family folklore and Mother still chuckles fondly about it to this day. I won't go into details. Suffice to say that the Ancestral Loos were put to good use that night. It's lucky we're all immortal.

"Get your hands out of there!" I demanded. Scarlettine had pulled open all my dressing-table drawers and was rummaging through them.

"No. I'm looking for a comb. Kissy-Woo's got a flea. Ah! Here's one!"

She held it up triumphantly. I shot out of bed, launched myself across the room, made a grab for the comb, missed and staggered out of control towards the door, which Frostia had thoughtfully left open to obtain the maximum draught. Scarlettine helped me through with a sisterly shove and Frostia kicked it shut.

The bolt shot across, and that was that.

I stood in the freezing corridor screaming abuse at them through the keyhole for a good ten minutes.

"You wait!" I screeched. "I'll get my own back, just you watch me! I wouldn't be in your shoes. Not for anything!"

Peals of mocking laughter from within. I finally admitted defeat and stormed off to the box room.

I lay there shivering, much too furious to sleep. Chucked out of my own bedroom on my own birthday! It was the last straw.

Well, I'd had enough. From now on, it was war.

There came a scratching at the door. I knew that sound. It was Denzil, Mrs Pudding's cat. He normally lives in the kitchen, but gets lonely when it's Bingo night.

Grateful at the thought of some company, I hauled myself out of bed and opened the door. In he came, all pleased and purring around my chilled ankles. He was already on the bed before I realized he had something in his mouth. It was a dead mouse.

All things considered, it was the most interesting present I received that night.

## 3. BREAKFAST

"Oh," I said, slouching into the breakfast room the following morning. "Still here then."

They were too. Frostia was sipping from a glass of iced milk and Scarlettine was munching on a red apple and feeding sausages to Kissy-Woo. They both looked up and sneered. Kissy-Woo bared her teeth and growled.

I say it was morning, but proper daylight hadn't actually arrived yet, because Mother was still up, having just got back from The Round. It's always gloomy when Mother's awake. The only time we get any decent daylight is during the few hours in the morning when she sleeps. Our candle bills are very high.

"Morning, pet," said Daddy. He was banging the up-ended sauce bottle on the table in an attempt to squeeze out the last brown globule. "Sleep well?"

"No," I said bitterly. "I didn't." I pointed an accusing finger. "*They* came and . . ."

"Honestly, Wilma," sighed Mother. "Do you have to wear that disgusting old dressing gown to the breakfast table? And you haven't even combed your hair. Look at your lovely sisters. Try and learn by their example."

"More coffee, ma'am?" inquired Peevish, crawling up in slow motion with a steaming pot. Peevish is very old. I wouldn't be surprised if he held some sort of record. I asked him once to what he attributed his old age. He told me the fact that he was born a long time ago and slammed the pantry door in my face. That's the kind of treatment I get around here.

"No thank you, Peevish," said Mother. "I don't want to be up all day. Do you need some more sauce, George?"

"D'you know, I believe I do," said Daddy, peering down the neck of the bottle.

"A fresh bottle of brown sauce for His Majesty, Peevish. Will you have some more sausages, dear?"

"D'you know, I believe I will." Daddy's partial to a nice fry-up.

"More sausages for the King, Peevish. And see if Lord Bacchus wants a cup of tea taking up, would you?"

"Right away, ma'am."

"Is the Queen Mother joining us this morning, do you know?"

"No, ma'am. She's rung for her sprouts to be brought up to the belfry, I believe."

"Oh. That's a shame. I was hoping she might come to say goodbye to the girls."

"Going soon then, are they? Good," I said, helping myself to scrambled egg.

"Wilma! Will you *please* stop that! I just don't know what gets into you sometimes."

"You haven't seen my room," I said darkly.

I had poked my nose into my bedroom on the way past. It was as I thought. Completely and utterly trashed. All my clothes had been pulled out of the wardrobe and dumped in a heap. My dressing table was awash with spilled make-up and old tissues. There were several more damp patches on the carpet, courtesy of Kissy-Woo. When I pulled back the covers of my bed, I found it occupied by a large, melting snowman with a label around its neck reading *BOO!* My Grade Three Magic certificate, of which I am rightly proud, was in the bin, along with the remains of my birthday cake.

"Why? What's wrong with your room?" inquired Mother tiredly.

"They've trashed it, that's what. It's in a complete and utter *state*, Mother."

"Oh yes?" piped up Scarlettine. "As if it's ever anything else, *Wilma*. Honestly, Mother. She does tell lies, doesn't she, Frosty?"

"We tried to tidy it," yawned Frostia. "But I'm afraid it was a hopeless task."

"I don't think Wilma *deserves* a nice room like that. I think she should move into a smaller one. Then we can have it when we stay over. We'd take care of it, wouldn't we, Frosty? After all, it used to be ours."

"They do have a point, you know, Wilma," said Mother. "There's no point in having a lovely big room like that if you're going to turn it into a slum."

I couldn't believe my ears. They were actually proposing to take my *bedroom* away! I opened my mouth to protest, but Mother was rising and glancing at her watch – a slim thing with a totally black face and no hands. It's a mystery how she tells the time with it.

"Well," she said, with a little yawn, "you'll have to excuse me. I'm off to bed. Some of us have to be up at sundown. Goodbye, darlings. Lovely to see you. Don't forget you're coming next weekend for my lunch party."

What? They were coming *again*?

"Goodbye, Mother," chorused Scarlettine and Frostia. "Sleep well."

"I will. Don't work too hard, George. Say goodbye to Bacchus for me when he gets up, and remind him about lunch next weekend. *Do* change out of that horrid dressing gown, Wilma. And try to do something about your hair."

And with that, she swept from the room.

Peevish creaked in with more sausages.

"I'll have a couple of those," I said.

"Honestly, Wilma, you're so *greedy*," said Scarlettine. "It's no wonder you're so dumpy. You'd better lose some weight before you become a Queen. By the way, have you decided yet what your title will be when you grow up?"

"None of your business," I snapped. Actually, I hadn't a clue. Most of the best titles have already been taken.

"I know what she can be Queen of," remarked

Frostia, crunching on an ice cube. "Queen of the Doughnuts. She ate enough at tea yesterday."

"No, no!" squealed Scarlettine, rocking with laughter. "I've got a better one! Queen of Puddings!"

"Tell them, Daddy," I ground out through gritted teeth.

"Come on now, girls," sighed Daddy. "Let's all be nice to each other, eh?"

We all stared at him. *Nice* to each other? *Us? Nice?*

"Sweet Daddy," said Scarlettine, reaching over and patting him on his bald head. "You just don't get it, do you? We're Wicked Queens. We don't *do* nice."

Peevish tottered to the window and pulled back the curtains. Sunshine streamed in. Outside, the birds began to sing. Over in one of the stables, Frostia's wolves started howling.

"Right," said Daddy, jumping up. "Your mother's asleep. Best catch the daylight, eh? I've got a lot to do out in the garden. Got a new boy coming for an interview."

"I suppose I'd better be getting along too," said Scarlettine. "I've got some new suitors coming today to claim my hand in marriage. Ah me! More flowers and chocolates. It's so tiresome, being beautiful and popular. Have *you* got any suitors coming today, Frosty?"

"No," drawled Frostia. "I haven't got time. I've got three blizzards to do and I'm horribly behind on my avalanches. Some of us have got better things to do than rush around looking for rich husbands."

"I don't rush around," said Scarlettine smugly. "I just

lie on a silken couch and let them come to me. Of course, they don't get past the door unless I've seen a copy of their bank statements. Come on, Kissy-Woo, home time. Tell Muckbucket to have my carriage brought round, would you, Peevish?"

"And my sleigh," added Frostia, unfolding like an ironing board. "Goodbye, Daddy. See you next weekend."

And with that, they all went their separate ways, leaving me to finish up the sausages.

I didn't bother to clear up my room. All that cake and snow and dog's puddles. Let the maids do it, I thought. I just selected my oldest dress from the pile on the floor, threw it on and made my way to the kitchen in the hopes that Mrs Pudding might be making gingerbread. I passed Peevish on his way up to Uncle Bacchus with something fizzing in a glass that didn't look much like tea.

Uncle Bacchus doesn't actually live with us, but tends to show up at meal times. He's the God of Wine and lives in an untidy castle on some goat-infested island where they grow grapes. Mother worries about him because he lives on takeaway kebabs and always has a lot of crates piled up on the doorstep. He's not her real brother. I think Grandma adopted him – goodness knows why. It's all a bit confusing and nobody talks about it much.

"I wouldn't go in there if I were you, Miss Wilma," warned Peevish, with a nod at the kitchen door. "She's having one of her days. She lost."

Oh.

We're all terrified of Mrs Pudding. Her moods veer from mildly grumpy to black raging fury, depending on how well she does at the Bingo.

Sure enough, the door suddenly burst open and a small maid flew past, sobbing into her apron. Doubtfully, I peered in. Mrs Pudding was on her knees, grimly scrubbing at the floor, muttering something about if you wanted a thing doing properly you might as well do it yourself. She looked up and saw me.

"Don't you come in here, mind!" she snapped curtly. "I'm not havin' you in here, dirtyin' up my floor with your great feet."

"I was just wondering . . ."

"Did you hear me?"

"But I just wanted to say thanks for the . . ."

Crash! The door slammed shut in my face.

". . . soap," I muttered.

"Told you," said Peevish, sounding rather smug, and continued on up the stairs.

That was that, then. No gingerbread. Disconsolately, I wandered back along the echoing corridors, wondering what to do with myself. My choices were:

**1.** I could go down to the dungeons and practice my Magical Arts. I have a laboratory set up down there. It's the perfect place – dark, damp and infested with rats, spiders and cockroaches. As anyone who knows about these things will tell you, Magic works much more effectively in the right setting.

**2.** I could go and poke about in the attic. It's

surprising what you can find up there. Glass slippers, seven league boots, broomsticks, rusty cauldrons – you name it, it's in our attic somewhere.

**3.** I could amuse myself with my new birthday gifts, i.e. take my lemon soap and lie in the bath brushing my hair and knitting a scarf for my new wetting doll whilst reading *A Thousand Years of Cutlery*. The mouth organ, of course, was no more.

**4.** I could go for a stroll in the garden and think about getting Revenge on my beastly sisters.

Having thought about my choices, I decided that there was no point in doing any Magic Practice. I was getting low on all the essential ingredients and might as well wait until the new stuff arrived from the catalogue. I'd had a feeling I wouldn't get what I wanted for my birthday, so I'd ordered it myself the week before, using three months' worth of saved allowance plus some extra money Mother had given me for shampoo. I didn't fancy the attic either. It gets too stuffy up there when the sun shines on the roof. As for the entertainment value of my grotty birthday presents . . .

I decided to go for a stroll in the garden.

# 4. ALVIS

It was a lovely day and the estate was looking its best. I stood at the top of the front steps and looked around. The driveway curved away into the trees in the distance. Rolling lawns stretched as far as the eye could see. Several gardeners were hurrying around with shears and hoses. Everyone always jumps to it when Mother's asleep, because it's so much easier to do chores in proper daylight and you never can be sure how long it's going to last. You can always tell when she's waking up because the sun goes in and the sky immediately starts to darken.

I was just debating which way to go, when I noticed a lanky youth coming up the driveway, looking vague and peering at a piece of paper in his hand. He was wearing the strangest selection of garments I have ever seen. His top half was draped with a large, loose, knee-length jacket made of some glittery fabric. His skinny legs were encased in tight black trousers. Goodness knows how he bent at the knees. Probably some sort of built-in hinge system. His shoes had unusually thick soles and were bright blue. The strangest thing about him, though, was his hair. It was slicked back, apart from a greasy forelock which dangled in his eyes.

I walked down the steps and went to meet him.

"Yes?" I said. It's rare to see strangers wandering about the grounds.

"Hey," he said. "How's it going?"

"Can I help you?" I said. "This is private property, you know."

"Yeah, right. Ancestral Halls of the Queen of the Night. You her maid or something?"

"Actually, I'm her daughter. Princess Wilma. And who might you be?"

"Alvis. Alvis Parsley. I've come about the job."

"Job? What job?"

"Er – what was it again?" He consulted his piece of paper. "Oh. Yeah. Gardener's boy."

"Oh, *right*. You want Daddy. You'll find him in the potting shed, I expect. Round the back, past the belfry, behind the stables. I suppose I could show you. I'm going that way myself."

"Cool."

"Is it? I thought it was quite warm for the time of year."

"No, I mean cool. Far out. You know."

I hadn't the slightest idea what he was talking about. We set out, me leading the way and him loping along behind, humming and clicking his fingers. He had a curious walk. His feet did a kind of rhythmic, shuffling dance, as though they were moving to the beat of some weird, distant drum.

"Hey!" he remarked, as we walked past the tulip bed. "Neat roses."

"You'll probably need some different clothes if you're going to be gardening," I said over my shoulder.

"Really? I've only got these. Won't they do?"

"Well, they're not very practical, are they? For slopping about in mud."

"Hey. Problem time." Alvis was sounding worried. "Think it'll matter? I really need this job, you dig?"

"No," I said, puzzled. "I don't dig. You're the gardener's boy. You'll be doing the digging. But I shouldn't worry," I added, seeing his distressed expression. "I'm sure Daddy will kit you out with something."

We rounded the corner and I pointed out the stables. Clint and Horace were out loose in the yard, waiting to begin the time-honoured ritual of kicking Muckbucket, the head groom, when he tried to rub them down after their hard night's ride. Clint and Horace pull the Night Coach – a sinister, all-black affair which Mother uses for The Round. They do all the normal horse-type things – lash out, spit hay, bite you when your back's turned and so on – with the added advantage that they can fly. Just as well, seeing that they need to circle the globe in a matter of hours.

We have other coaches and horses, of course, but only Clint and Horace are used for The Round. Nobody touches them apart from Mother and Muckbucket. Well, who'd want to?

"That's Clint and Horace," I told Alvis warningly. "Don't go near them, whatever you do. They'll trample you as soon as look at you . . ."

I broke off. To my surprise and consternation, Clint and Horace had raised their heads and were looking in our direction. Then, with one accord, they both came cantering over. I backed away, but Alvis hung over the fence and gave a little whistle.

"Get back!" I shouted. "They're after us! They . . ."

My voice trailed away. Clint was nuzzling Alvis's pocket. Horace had placed his huge head on Alvis's shoulder. They both had soppy looks on their faces.

"Hey!" said Alvis. "Hi there, fellers." He reached in his pocket and brought out two lumps of sugar, which he proceeded to feed to them. They didn't even nip his fingers, let alone take his arm off.

I was dumbfounded. I'd never seen Clint and Horace do that before. They were very good in the wild-eye-rolling and the mad-tossing-of-the-mane department, but all this soppy stuff was new.

"Cool horses," observed Alvis, stroking their noses.

"Mm. Do you know about horses, then, er – Alvis?"

"Nope. Ma's got a donkey, though. Pulls the caravan."

He took a comb out of his pocket and proceeded to slick back his hair, which Horace was affectionately trying to chew. Just then, Muckbucket came out of the stables with a couple of clanking pails. He looked over and stopped short, mouth open.

"Off you go then, guys," said Alvis, giving Clint and Horace a couple of brisk pats on their rumps. They turned and went trotting back to their stable, good as gold. Muckbucket, looking dazed, opened the doors and they went in. He gave Alvis a puzzled look, then followed them, slamming the door behind him.

"Is that the potting shed?" asked Alvis, pointing. "That little hut over there? By that – hey, what's it called – bush?"

I stared at him. "You don't know much about gardening, do you, Alvis?" I said.

"No," he admitted. "Not much. We're on the road a lot, Ma and me. Don't stop anywhere long enough to grow stuff." He finished arranging his oily coil and put the comb away. "How do I look?"

Well, what was I to say?

"Fine," I said. "Very – er – fine."

"Will I get the job, though?"

"Oh, sure to."

"Great!" he said cheerfully. "Hey, nice meeting you. I was feeling nervous, you know? I feel better now."

"No need to feel nervous of Daddy," I told him. "He's not like the rest of us. He's sweet."

"And the rest of you aren't?"

"No," I told him truthfully. "We're not. We're pretty sinister, on the whole. We dabble with dark powers. It's a kind of – hobby."

"Is that right?" he said, interested, then adding, "Me, I play guitar."

"Really?" I said. "Well, each to his own. I'll leave you now then. One tip. Admire his tomatoes. Those are the small green round things in the pots."

"Yeah? I always thought tomatoes were supposed to be big and red."

"Not Daddy's," I said firmly.

"Oh. Right. OK. Tomatoes are small green things. I'll remember that. Anything else?"

"Tulips are yellow straight things. Roses aren't. Good luck."

"Got it. Hey! Thanks, Wilma. See you around." He gave me a grin and went loping off.

I wondered whether to call him back and explain that he should address me as Your Royal Highness or, at the very least, *Miss* Wilma – then decided against it. He had enough to worry about as it was, what with having only the one outfit of odd clothes and never living long in one place. Time enough to explain about correct behaviour if he got the job – which I doubted he would, despite my useful gardening tips. In all likelihood, I'd probably never see him again.

I turned and was about to head off in the direction of the orchard, when I heard a tapping noise coming from above my head. It was Grandma. She was standing at the window of the belfry, banging on the glass with her stick and making urgent beckoning signs. Oh dear.

I don't go up to Grandma's often. It's serious spooky time. Officially, she is head of the Family, but she leaves leaves everything to Mother these days, preferring to spend most of her time up with the bats in the belfry, where she has a granny flat. She's very doomy, is Grandma. Trying to get a smile out of her is like forcing sugar from vinegar. The only time she emerges is on important family occasions, when she either falls asleep or sits around shouting for sprouts. Yes, you heard me. Sprouts. That's all she ever eats. Don't ask me why. It's another one of those grim family secrets that nobody ever talks about. I asked Mother about it once and she changed the subject.

The belfry is a tall, dark, ivy-covered tower which stands apart from the main bulk of the Ancestral Halls. Many years ago it had a bell, but that got removed when Grandma decided she wanted to live there. There are still bats there though. There used to be hundreds, but most of them had to go because of the droppings. Now there are only three. Pat, Matt and Hatty. They're not my idea of pets, but they suit Grandma. She's a bit like a bat herself. When I was little, I used to wonder whether she hung upside down when she went to sleep.

With a little sigh, I entered the small wooden door at the base of the belfry and began the long climb up the winding stairway. It went on – and on – and on. Much, much more than it should have, considering the height of the belfry viewed from outside. It's high, but not *that* high.

I finally reached the top and knocked on the forbidding little door. Then I took a deep breath and stepped in.

There is something odd about Grandma's room. From the outside, the belfry looks extremely narrow, but the room Grandma occupies is really quite sizeable. That's because Magic was used in its construction. Only Magic can make a place bigger on the inside than it is out.

Like most old people's rooms, it is packed with over-large furniture. There is a massive, carved wardrobe, filled with identical rusty black frocks, shawls and ancient pairs of leather button boots. There are overstuffed armchairs and bow-legged tables set out like an obstacle course. Every single surface is piled high with old, yellowing newspapers. Grandma takes all the papers every day and never throws any away. Cobwebs hang from the rafters and the walls are hung with Family portraits in heavy gilt frames. We're all there: Mother, Daddy, Uncle Bacchus, my sisters and me.

The seventh painting is turned to the wall. It's always been that way, as long as I can remember. It's never occurred to me to ask why. Another one of life's little mysteries. Perhaps I would ask her. It would be something to talk about if the conversation flagged.

A saggy old four-poster occupies one shadowy corner. A tall grandfather clock stands in another. It ticks, but the hands always stay at twelve. The third corner has a bookcase full of crumbling books. A suit of armour stands in the fourth. A small sink occupies the fifth.

Yes. You heard me. There is a fifth corner. I told you the place was odd.

There is no bath, because Grandma doesn't hold with it. She only bathes once a year, on New Year's

Day, when you see the servants struggling up the stairs with a copper tub and jugs full of hot water while Grandma stands at the top in an old black dressing gown, waving her stick and shouting abuse. That's just one of her little ways.

Right now, she was sitting in her rocking chair like a small, hunched crow. Her stick was placed across her knees. Pat, Matt and Hatty were hanging from the curtain rail. They flew up in a panic when I entered the room and started flapping wildly about.

"That's enough, you three. Hang!" commanded Grandma. Rather sulkily, they returned to the rail and hung.

"Hello, Grandma," I said, rather breathless from all that climbing.

She turned and stared at me with her hooded eyes. "Who was that you were talkin' to, girl?" she demanded.

"No one important. Just some boy come about a gardening job. Did you want something?"

"Why should I *want* somethin'?" she demanded testily. "Can't you come up and see your old grandma sometimes without me *wantin'* somethin'?"

"Oh. Right. Yes, of course." I looked around the room for somewhere to sit. The armchairs were out because of the papers. In the end, I perched on the end of the bed.

"Thanks for the birthday present, by the way," I said.

"What birthday present?"

"The Junior Knitting Kit."

"I didn't get you no *knittin' kit*," she spat. "Since when do the girls in this Family need darned fool *knittin' kits*. Your mother must've got it and wrote my name on. When was your birthday anyway?"

"Yesterday. I was twelve. You came to tea, remember?"

"Oh. I was wonderin' what all that was about. I think I might have dozed off."

A silence fell. The grandfather clock ticked. Pat, Matt and Hatty hung. I swung my legs and tried not to yawn. I thought she had dropped off again and was just thinking about creeping out when she spoke.

"Did you like it, then? The *knittin' kit* what I didn't get you?"

"No," I said. "Not much."

"I'm not surprised. Swine of a present. If they'd given me a knittin' kit when I was twelve, I'd have chucked it back in their faces and zapped 'em with a lightnin' bolt."

"Would you?" I said, with curiosity. It was hard to imagine Grandma ever having been twelve.

"Too right. I was already in trainin' to be Night Queen when I was twelve. They didn't hang about in them days. None o' this waitin' until you comes of age nonsense. They put me to work, my girl. And quite right too. I had my Grade Six Magic when I was your age. The year after, I was out doin' The Round. Oh yes. It was different then. None o' this mollycoddlin'."

"Really?" I said, wide-eyed. Grandma didn't usually volunteer this much information. "Go on. Tell me more about when you were a girl."

"Nah," said Grandma shortly. "Nothin' more to tell." She nodded at the tray sitting on a small table next to her. "Take them dishes down with you. An' tell Puddin' to boil the sprouts for twenty minutes next time. Twenty, not fifteen. I keep tellin' her I likes 'em mushy. That last lot was harder'n bullets."

"But I thought you wanted some company . . ."

"Well, I don't. I wants quiet. Go on, girl. Clear off."

I stood and picked up the tray. Then I paused.

"Just one thing, Grandma," I said.

"What?"

"That picture. The one on the wall. Who is it *of*? Why is it facing the other way? I've always wanted to know . . ."

I broke off. She was on her feet, wizened face contorted and stick pointed at me.

*ZAP!*

A bolt of green light shot from the end of the stick, missing my left ear by inches and removing a large chunk of plaster from the wall behind. Pat, Matt and Hatty took off from the curtain rail and flapped dementedly about my head. Thoroughly alarmed, I dropped the tray. Bowls and cutlery went crashing to the floor.

*"Out!"* she screeched. *"Comin' up here with your darned fool questions! Out, d'you hear?"*

I didn't stop to argue. I turned and raced from the room, stumbling back down the stairs with her shrieks still ringing in my ears.

"I don't understand it," I complained to Daddy. It was

ten minutes later. I was sitting in the potting shed, dabbing at my knee with his hanky. I had fallen down the last four stairs and was bleeding quite profusely. "I mean, she invites me up there, then she turns into a mad woman and tries to zap me with her stick! It's a good thing she's short-sighted."

"I don't know, Wilma," sighed Daddy. He was pottering about, clipping dead leaves off his tomato plants with a pair of scissors. "You must have said something to upset her, pet."

"But we were getting on *fine*. She was telling me all about her life when she was a girl. Then I asked her about the seventh painting, and she . . ."

"You did *what*?" Daddy looked up, startled.

"I asked her about the painting. You know, the one that's turned to the wall?"

"Oh dear," said Daddy. "Now you've gone and done it. No wonder she had one of her turns."

"But *why*?"

Daddy flopped heavily on to the bench.

"How old are you, Wilma?" he asked.

"Twelve. It was my birthday yesterday, Daddy. You'd think *somebody* would remember."

"Twelve, eh? Well, I suppose it's time you knew."

"Knew *what*?"

"About your missing Aunt Maud."

"Who?"

"Maud. Your mother's sister."

"Mother's *sister*? I didn't know she *had* a sister."

"No. Well, you wouldn't. We don't talk about her, you see. Her name's mud."

"I thought it was Maud?"

"No, what I mean is, no one's allowed to mention it. Grandma's orders. Listen, if I tell you, you don't say a word, right?"

"Right," I breathed. I was all ears. Secrets were to be revealed. Daddy went to the doorway, peered out, then carefully shut the door. Then he sat back on the bench and began to speak in low, confidential tones.

"It was like this," he said. "Your grandma had two children. Veronica, your mother, and Maud. Maud was the eldest, and a bit of a rebel, by all accounts. Always neglecting her lessons, an' off dancing round maypoles and talking to trees. When your grandma retired, it was Maud who was supposed to take over the title of Queen of the Night. But Maud had other plans. On the night of her coronation, she upped and ran away with the gypsies. Couldn't face going into the Family business, I suppose. It's not everybody who's cut out for it."

"Oh," I said. "I *see*."

"Your mother was very cut up about it. Fond of her sister, she was. Wanted to find her and bring her home. Or at least find out what had become of her. But your grandma wouldn't hear of it. Maud had turned her back on the Family and that was it." He gave a little sigh. "She's a hard woman, your grandma. Mind you, she did adopt Uncle Bacchus as company for your mother. He was supposed to have been a girl, but the adoption agency got it wrong. Your grandma tried to send him back when she discovered the mistake, but they wouldn't have him." Daddy gave a little chortle.

"Anyway, your mother had got attached to him. Gave her something to take her mind off things."

"So Mother took over? As Queen of the Night?"

"Eventually. But that wasn't plain sailing either. She'd met me, you see. Your grandma didn't think I was good enough for her, me being a commoner. Grandma had arranged for her to marry the King of the Underworld, but your mother wasn't having it. She said he had sticky-out ears. So your mother and I eloped."

*"Eloped? Really?"*

"Yes. Your mother's coronation had to be put back and everything. Shocking fuss. Your grandma's never been the same since. Well, I suppose it did come as a bit of a shock, after Maud running off like that. It turned her a bit – well, you know."

"Wow!" I said. All this family history was a lot to take in at one go. "So no one knows what became of Aunt Maud?"

"Nope. One night there, the next night gone. With the gypsies. That's Maud for you."

"What was their name? The gypsies?"

Daddy looked at me with a wry little smile.

"Sprout," he said. "They was known as the Sprouts."

Aha! At long last, Grandma's strange food fixation made sense.

"Anyway," said Daddy, with a little sigh. "Anyway, it all happened a long time ago. That's enough skeletons in the cupboard for one day. I don't know about you, but I'm ready for a cuppa. Care to join me?" He reached for the battered old kettle he keeps in the shed.

"Yes, please," I said. A thought suddenly struck me. "By the way, how did the boy get on with his interview? Did you hire him?"

"What, young Alvis? Yes. Starting tomorrow morning. Seemed very keen. Very interested in my tomatoes. Odd clothes he was wearing, mind. Strange hair too. That *coiled spring* effect at the front. How does he do that, d'you suppose?"

There was a little pause while we both considered the mystery of Alvis Parsley's hair. Then Daddy started talking about his tomato plants and I hastily drank my tea and departed.

By this time, I was feeling peckish. I wandered back inside and made for the kitchen. Mrs Pudding had got over her bad mood and was making gingerbread after all. I spent the afternoon eating it and cuddling Denzil.

Of course, sorting out the new gardening boy and getting zapped by Grandma and hearing the history of my missing Aunt Maud was all very interesting – but a whole day had gone by and I hadn't even *started* planning my revenge on Scarlettine and Frostia. I couldn't let missing relations distract me.

Revenge first. I'd get cracking on that, first thing tomorrow.

# 5. DOWN IN THE DUNGEONS

The following morning, the package from the catalogue company arrived. Yesssss! I simply couldn't wait to open it.

"Smells a bit whiffy," observed the postman. He wasn't our regular one or he would have been used to it.

"That'll be the Essential Skunk Oil," I told him.

"Ha, ha, ha!" chortled the postman, shaking his head as he went off down the drive. "You're such a joker, Your Highness." Little did he know. He obviously hadn't heard about our Family. We've got quite a reputation at the post office.

I took the dungeon key from the hook by the front door. You can get down to the dungeons from inside the Ancestral Halls, but it meant going through the kitchen. The parcel *was* rather smelly and I didn't fancy a confrontation with Mrs Pudding. She's fussy about what goes through her kitchen. It was easier to go out around the side and get to them that way.

I picked up the huge parcel and staggered down the steps. I rounded the corner and ran slap into Alvis, who was trundling a wheelbarrow along. It contained a great many leaves. Sitting on top, purring contentedly, was Denzil.

"Hello," I said.

"Hey," he said cheerfully. He was wearing a brown smock and big rubber boots. A straw hat covered his strange, greased-back hair – although the corkscrew still hung down in front.

"You got the job then?"

"Yep. Thanks for the tip about the tomatoes."

"You're welcome. Er, nice smock."

"Yeah. I miss my threads, but hey! Smocks can rock. Need a hand with that?" He pointed at my parcel.

"Well, yes. That would be nice." I wish I knew what he was talking about sometimes. "But don't you have jobs to do?

"They'll wait. I owe you a favour, right?"

He took the parcel from me and placed it in the wheelbarrow next to Denzil, who playfully reached out and grabbed his hand.

"He seems to like you," I remarked. Actually, I felt a bit miffed. I like to think that Denzil and I have a special relationship. Next to Mrs Pudding, I'm his favourite person – or have been, up until now.

"Yeah," said Alvis, tickling him under the chin. "Guess I take after Ma. She's got a way with animals. Where are you going with the parcel?"

"Down to the dungeons," I said. "That's where I have my secret laboratory. Follow me."

"Hey," said Alvis enthusiastically. "Dungeons. Secret lab. Cool."

The entrance to the dungeons is by way of a small, age-blackened oak door with a small barred grille set in the top half. It lies at the bottom of a steep flight of stone steps. I went down first to open it. Alvis came behind with the package, Denzil twining lovingly around his ankles. I fought with the padlock for a minute or too, then finally the door opened, hinges shrieking a shrill complaint.

Inside, it was as black as pitch.

"Whoooo!" said Alvis. "Spooky. Any ghosts?"

"One or two," I told him truthfully. "There's one with a chain who complains all the time and a green one who gibbers in corners. But I don't suppose we'll see them. They're not fond of me. Shut the door, I don't want Denzil coming in. He mucks about with all my stuff. And mind your head. There's a low archway a bit further along."

We set off along the winding corridor. As we passed, candles in niches sprang alight. That's because they're Magic candles. We use them upstairs. They're terribly expensive. I pinched them from the box Peevish keeps in the pantry.

"This is my laboratory," I announced, pushing open a set of doors. More Magic candles sensed my presence and flamed into life, dramatically lighting the scene within.

Although I say it myself, I've made quite a good job of the lab. It's not as untidy as my bedroom. I've got most of my stuff set out on proper racking: crucibles in one place, mascots and lucky charms in another, powders, potions and mystic herbs alphabetically arranged in labelled jars and so on. There are boxes containing wishbones, talismans, horseshoes and special chalks for drawing Magic Circles. I have a work bench all set up with my Bunsen burner and my microscope. I have shelves full of reference books. My Staff of Power and a couple of divining rods are neatly placed in an umbrella stand. There are cobwebs. There are echoes. There are drips. There is the obligatory stuffed crocodile hanging from a rafter. There is a packet of chocolate biscuits in a drawer for when I get peckish. Everything you need, really.

"Wow!" said Alvis, impressed. "Some place you got here."

"Put the package over there," I said, pointing to the bench. "Thanks."

"No problem. Anything else I can do?"

"No. *Don't touch that!*"

He was poking at the stuffed crocodile, which winked one glass eye and clashed its jaws together, narrowly missing his finger. Stuffed it might be. Friendly it wasn't.

"Wowee!" said Alvis. "Heavy! How does it work?"

"Just a simple animation charm. Look, I don't want

to keep you. I'm sure you've got jobs to do."

"Eh?" Alvis was peering around, clearly fascinated. "Oh. Yeah, right. I'll get going then. What exactly do you *do* here?"

"Well – Magic," I said. "Isn't it obvious?"

"Yeah? Hey, I'd love to see you do some Magic. What kind of Magic?"

"Stuff. You know. Right now, I'm thinking of Revenge Spells. I need to get my own back on my sisters."

"You've got sisters?"

"Sadly, yes. One's Queen of the Snow, the other's Queen of Mirrors."

"Is that right? How come you're not Queen of anything then?"

I was about to snap at him. I'm touchy about this particular subject. But he wasn't to know. He was just curious.

"I'm not old enough. You have to be seventeen before you get a title."

"Right. Why do you want to get revenge on them?"

"It's a long story," I said. "But I can assure you they deserve it."

"Fair enough. Are you going to get revenge on both of them at the same time or separately?"

"Probably separately. It's too complicated to do them both together."

"Which one will you do first?"

"I don't know yet." Why was he asking all these questions?

"What's that over there? The knobbly stick with the moon and stars and stuff? In the umbrella stand?"

"That's my Staff of Power."

"What about those tangled bits of string?"

"They're my Magic Cords. Look, I don't want to keep you."

"That's OK."

"No. I mean, I *really* don't want to keep you. You can go now. I've got things to do."

"Oh. Well, if you're sure there's nothing . . ."

"No," I said firmly. "If there is, I'll let you know. Make sure you shut the outer door."

"OK. Right. See you later." And, rather reluctantly, he departed, leaving me to open my package.

As always, the catalogue company (Magic Inc.) had got some of my order wrong. Instead of Frog's Bane, they had sent Toad's Blight, a vastly inferior product. They were out of Dodo Drops and Dried Fish Lips. However, the Essential Skunk Oil was there, together with Powdered Wartwood, Faraway Seeds, Goat Grains, Boggleweed, Salamander Spit, Plumbum Root, Marsh Mist, Tarantula Tears, Extract of Scorpion, and a large economy-size bottle of Squiffi Water.

At the bottom of the box, carefully wrapped in a black velvet cloth, was the new Crystal Ball. The one with audio facilities that I had coveted so long. The one that can see into the past, present and future. I was really looking forward to trying it out. My old one only did the future. It had belonged to Scarlettine and was worn out anyway. It took ages for the mists to clear, and the power had got so low that you could only see half an hour ahead. A couple of weeks before, I had dropped it on my toe and the immediate future had involved a lot of sticking plaster.

There was also a new wand. I was excited about that, too. My old one had developed an annoying fault. Whenever I waved it, the green sparks that issued from the tip crackled back along the length of the wand and up my arm, causing my hair to stand on end. Very unpleasant, plus it made me look silly.

There was a book too. *Ye Revenge Spelles* by Arbora Grudge. It's the third in a popular series, which includes *Creative Cursing* and *Ye Basic Brews*. I already had those.

I spent a pleasant half hour replenishing my jars and bottles, then tried out the new wand, which worked beautifully. I aimed it at the mouse which always hangs around the drawer where I keep my chocolate biscuits, muttered a simple changing spell and watched with satisfaction as it gave a brief, surprised squeak, then turned into a tortoise. Clean, quick and efficient. No sparks up the arm either. Excellent.

"That'll learn you," I muttered. It crawled off, looking rather confused.

I peered into the new Crystal Ball and thought about what I would be doing in half an hour's time. Instantly, the mists cleared and I observed myself, in miniature, talking to Alvis down in the walled garden, where he was hacking inexpertly at bushes with a pair of shears. It was a good, clear picture. Excellent definition. I considered trying out the audio facility, but decided against it. Alvis would probably be startled if he heard my voice coming at him out of thin air. The shears looked sharp. I didn't want him to cut his foot off. Also, what I was saying to him would be in the future and I would hear myself. I wasn't sure I could get my head around that.

Now to the book. I was looking forward to this. I took *Ye Revenge Spelles* and the packet of chocolate biscuits over to the old armchair I keep in the corner, curled up and began to read.

There were ten spells. Each was clearly laid out under five main headings: "Ye Spelle", "Ye Diagram", "Ye Recipe", "Ye Method" and "Ye Result". There were also handy safety tips about washing your hands and clearing the area in case of explosions and so on, but I skipped those. As I've already said, I've got my Grade Three. I can hardly be called a novice.

There was "Brother Mildew's Chronic Upheaval", which causes your victim to suffer from rather nasty tummy upsets.

There was "Old Mother Wiley's Agonizing Pricklefoot", which brings on shocking pins and needles the minute your victim swings his/her feet out of bed in the mornings.

There was "Granny Horlicks's Embarrasing Odour", which doesn't really need explaining.

There was "Malacarp's Excruciating Lump Accelerator", which causes boils.

There was "Wizard Tweedle's False Wing Syndrome", which gives the sufferer the illusion that he/she can fly.

There was "Gammer Gamelion's Treasure

Trivializer", where your victim is always broke, no matter how much money he/she makes.

There was "Humpdinkler's Extraordinary Swollen Knee", which – well, which causes an extraordinary swollen knee which hurts like mad, as well as looking daft.

The spell that caught my eye though was the author's own contribution. It was called "Arbora Grudge's Rite of Vanishment" and had the effect of making your victim's most beloved possession vanish into thin air, never to be seen again.

Aha!

The thing about Arbora's spells is that if you follow the recipe properly, they always come out right. This one sounded good. It wouldn't do for Frostia, of course. She doesn't have any beloved possessions. She has *things* – but nothing she really cares about. Scarlettine's different. She has lots of things she cares passionately about. Not for very long, mind. She soon gets tired of them. She's always getting new pets which she's crazy about for a week or two, then you never hear about them again. The only pet she's hung on to for any length of time is that waddling hairball, Kissy-Woo, who's still there despite a parade of kittens, ponies, boa constrictors and tarantulas. The trouble is, Kissy-Woo has a particular aversion to me. It wouldn't be easy to lure her away from Scarlettine. I would need help.

Ten minutes later, just as the Crystal Ball had foretold, I was talking to Alvis in the rose garden.

"Alvis," I said. "I wonder if I can have a word? I

think there *is* something you can help me out with after all. Remember I was telling you about getting my own back on my sisters? And how you said you'd like to see me do some Magic? Well, I can't help noticing you've got a way with animals, and I've been doing a bit of reading. Basically, I've got this *Plan* . . ."

# 6. THE LUNCH PARTY

Mother is famous for her lunch parties. She holds them once a month. She would have them more often, but The Round plays havoc with her social life, as she never tires of letting us know, and once a month is all she can manage.

I hung around the fringes and watched the guests arrive. Mother's friends come from all walks of Magic, Myth and Legend. Her three best cronies were there – the Queen of the Sea, the Queen of the Winds and the Storm Queen (privately known to Daddy and me as Soggy, Puffer and Rumbleguts.) Soggy is short and watery-eyed and tends to dress in flowing green and blue robes, which don't suit her a bit. Puffer always looks untidy and goes in for grey. Rumbleguts is flashy and wears loads of lipstick. She has enormous earrings and streaks of lightning embroidered on her robes.

"Oh, Wilma, dear!" cried Soggy, spotting me helping myself to nibbles from the sideboard. "My, what a *big* girl you're getting."

I glared at her. Normally, I avoid Mother's lunches like the plague, but I had to turn up to this one on account of my Plan.

"Hmm," said Puffer, examining me through her monocle. "She hasn't inherited her mother's beauty, that's for sure," she added in a loud undertone. "Horrible hair."

"Are your lovely sisters coming today?" put in Rumbleguts.

I was prevented from having to reply by a flurry of new arrivals, consisting of the Mountain King (a Dwarf in an iron crown); the Great God Pan (green, tends to play his pipes at every opportunity); Lady Luck and Lord Loser; Cupid (a daft little twit with cherubic curls and silly little wings); Mother Earth (large, brown kaftan); and the Tooth Fairy, wearing a horrible pink dress studded with thousands of little teeth that she claims to sew on by hand. Each new arrival had their own fanfare, so it was impossible to carry on a conversation over the blaring trumpets.

Grandma was already ensconced in her chair by the fire, where she sat hunched and brooding, irritably waving away anyone who had the nerve to come up and try talking to her. Uncle Bacchus and Daddy were chatting to the Sandman (who, like Mother, always looks tired because of the hours he works), the Lord of the Elves (hooked nose, pointy ears) and a minor woodland deity called Herne the Hunter (who has a gigantic pair of antlers spouting from his head and frequently gets mistaken for a hat stand). There was a lot of laughter and back-slapping going on in the men's crowd. The women were standing around waving their fans and eyeing up each other's dresses.

My sisters were late, as usual. They do it on purpose so that they can make a big, dramatic entrance. I noticed that Mother kept glancing anxiously at the clock as she glided about among her guests. Lunch was a hot buffet, due to be served up at twelve o'clock precisely. Mrs Pudding had her team of kitchen staff all lined up and ready to bring in the food. It was now ten past and there was still no sign. The plates containing the nibbles were emptying fast and quite a few of the guests were beginning to glance at their watches.

Then, there was another fanfare, and there they were.

Frostia was looking even more hatchet-faced than usual, I noticed. Something had happened to put her out. Scarlettine was at her brightest, most vivacious, most nauseating worst. She wore a red velvet gown, trimmed with rubies. Her matching accessories included a ruby tiara, a red velvet muff, elbow-length gloves and Kissy-Woo, whose fat little body was squeezed into a stupid-looking red velvet coatee trimmed with pompoms.

"Frostia's sleigh lost a runner, can you believe?" cried Scarlettine to the assembled company. "I had to stop off and give her a lift. That's why we're late! I had to make a detour to the North Pole! Brrr. Let me get to the fire! I'm freezing!"

"Darlings!" trilled Mother. "There you are! Peevish, you can tell Mrs Pudding to send in the food now. The girls have arrived."

In seconds, Frostia and Scarlettine were surrounded by admirers, all competing to take their cloaks and provide them with drinks. It really was quite sickening.

"Frostia, darling, you're looking quite lovely today," said Mother. "*Do* tell us all what you've been doing."

"Just the usual," drawled Frostia. "I've been having a bit of trouble with the polar icecaps. They're melting, you know. Such a bore. But I *did* find time to do a spot of kidnapping. Some small boy in a town I was passing through."

"*Really?* How exciting. Did you hear that, everyone? Frostia's kidnapped a *boy*."

There was a round of applause from the assembled guests, who mostly thought that kidnapping was a very fine thing to do.

"I don't know," sighed Daddy, shaking his head. "You girls. That's not very nice, Frostia."

"Well, he hooked his toboggan on to my sleigh. What does he expect?"

"But his family will worry about him, pet. How would you feel if our Wilma was kidnapped?"

"Thrilled," said Frostia.

"But . . ."

"George, go and help Peevish see to the drinks, will you?" Mother butted in. She blew Daddy a kiss and gave him a firm little push. This was Wicked Queen stuff. He couldn't be expected to understand. Sighing, he wandered off.

"What do you intend doing with the little fellow, darling?" inquired Mother brightly.

"I don't know," shrugged Frostia. "He's rather boring actually. Keeps complaining of chilblains. I've left him back in the palace trying to make words with lumps of ice."

"You'll be able to teach him Scrabble," said Puffer, nodding approvingly.

Scarlettine was getting annoyed. I could tell. It was clear that she felt Frostia had held centre stage long enough. She set down Kissy-Woo and elbowed aside a couple of guests who were in her way.

"Actually, *I've* got some news," she announced. "Step aside, Frostia, if you please. I have an announcement to make that'll knock *your* news into a cocked hat."

All eyes were on her as, slowly, she peeled off her left glove and held out her hand. On her finger was a huge ruby ring. It flashed in the candlelight, bringing forth an awed gasp from the assembled company.

"Oh, darling!" gasped Mother. "Is that what I think it is?"

"It's an engagement ring," announced Scarlettine, smugness oozing from every pore. "I'm going to be married."

Ooohs, aaaahs and a storm of clapping followed this announcement. Even Frostia's kidnapped boy couldn't compete with this. Daft little Cupid took off and flew around the chandelier, spraying everyone with ludicrous hearts as he always does at the slightest hint of romance.

"Who's the lucky man, niece?" bellowed Uncle Bacchus, waving his bottle around.

"King Geraldo of Truss," simpered Scarlettine.

There was a united gasp. Even *I* had heard of King Geraldo of Truss. He was a hugely rich widower who lived in a gigantic palace that was almost as big as the Ancestral Halls. Money to flush away, as Grandma would say.

"*Scarlettine!*" cried Mother, all of a flutter. "*Darling!* What a *catch*! Did you hear that, everybody?"

"What did you do?" murmured Frostia. "Put a love potion in his drink?"

"Shut up, Frosty, you're only jealous! Anyway, as I was *saying*, he swore never to marry again when his first wife died, but of course, he hadn't met *me* then. He's got some stupid daughter called Snow Drop or Snow Plough or something, but I don't suppose she'll bother us much. We can always confine her to a tower with a doll until she's seventeen. Then we can marry her off and she'll be out of our hair."

"Now, now, Scarlettine, that's not the way to talk," began the lone voice of Daddy, but just then the doors opened and Mrs Pudding's staff entered bearing smoking tureens and silver platters heaped high with food. The males in the party made a beeline for the sideboard and began politely fighting for plates and cutlery. The females gathered around Scarlettine and Frostia, chattering excitedly. An engagement and a kidnapping all in one day. What could be more exciting?

Now, normally, I admit it, I would have been first in the food queue – but not today. I had the Plan, you see. All the time that Scarlettine and Frostia had been hogging the limelight, I had been keeping a close eye on Kissy-Woo. The wretched animal had been waddling about amongst people's legs, growling at ankles and hoovering up dropped nibbles.

Right now, she was snuffling around over by the main entrance. Everybody's back was turned. This was the ideal time.

Casually, I walked over and pushed open the door. Kissy-Woo felt the draught and looked up. I reached into my pocket and brought out the newspaper parcel I had prepared earlier. It contained a chop bone. I had sneaked into the kitchen earlier and pinched it when Mrs Pudding had her back turned.

"Here, Kissy-Woo," I whispered. "What's this Wilma's got for you?"

Kissy-Woo stared at me suspiciously and growled. We loathe each other. She knows that.

"Come on," I cooed encouragingly. "It's a lovely, lovely chop bone. Don't you want it?"

I waved it about under her nose. I don't think she'd ever seen a bone before. Her diet consists mainly of chocolate, which accounts for the fact that she looks like a walking bed-roll. Ancient dog instinct clicked in and she began to slaver. Her jaws opened. I moved backwards, waggling the bone. She waddled towards me. I moved back again, keeping the bone just out of her reach.

I backed out and placed it on the top step. She stood in the doorway, undecided, looking from the bone to me, then back to the bone again. As arranged, Alvis was waiting at the bottom, leaning against a stone pillar and humming.

"Over to you, Alvis," I said. "Let's see if you can work your charm on this one."

"Hey," said Alvis, patting his knees. "Hi there, little dog. Who's a lovely girl then?"

His words had a magical effect. Kissy-Woo's ears pricked up. Ignoring both me and the bone, she bounced down the steps, tail wagging. Alvis knelt down and held his arms open. She jumped into them with a glad little woof and began delightedly licking his face.

"Good girl," crooned Alvis, tickling her tummy. "Hey, she's cute."

"No she isn't," I said, disgusted. "She's an over-fed little monster."

"You're not going to hurt her, are you?" said Alvis, suddenly anxious. "Because I couldn't be party to that . . ."

"No, of course not. I'm just going to give her her first taste of real fresh air. Come on. Let's go."

# 7. THE RITE OF VANISHMENT

Down in the lab, everything was prepared. The Magic Circle was drawn. It had taken me ages to get it right. The dungeon floor is rather uneven and it kept ending up as a Magic Oblong. The outline had been sprinkled with the appropriate herbs and candles placed at all four points of the compass.

I draped myself with lucky medallions, pinned on a few talismans and added a couple of rabbit's feet for luck.

"Hey," said Alvis. "Cool jewels." He was sitting cross-legged on the floor, playing with Kissy-Woo. They were having a jolly game of tug of war, using the black velvet cloth which came with my new Crystal Ball. Kissy-Woo had one end in her mouth and was shaking it madly from side to side and pretending to growl. I had never seen her do anything remotely dog-like before. Alvis brought out the best in her.

"They're Magical Amulets," I told him, adding, "Look, *must* you do that with my highly expensive cloth? She's getting slobber all over it."

"She's enjoying herself. She doesn't get enough exercise."

I sighed and opened *Ye Revenge Spelles* at the relevant page. I had read it so often I knew it by heart, but Alvis didn't – and I was going to need his assistance. The "Rite of Vanishment" includes an Incantation, you see, and Incantations work so much better when there are two of you. It doubles the Power. Also, quite frankly, one feels a bit silly, standing around all on one's own spouting bad poetry. The embarrassment gets in the way of the Magic.

"Right," I said. "I'm ready to begin. Stick her in the Circle. Don't step over the edge yourself, whatever you do."

Alvis jumped to his feet, scooped up Kissy-Woo and placed her in the Circle, together with the velvet cloth. Finding herself the sole possessor, she jumped on it triumphantly and began to rip it to shreds.

"I need your help with the Incantation," I said.

"What's that?"

"It's a sort of rhyme."

"What, like, 'Baa baa black sheep'?"

"No. Well, yes, sort of. Are you helping or aren't you?"

"OK." Amiably, he loped up and peered over my

shoulder. "What's that brown stuff on the page? Mystic paste or something?"

"Chocolate biscuit. Look, we haven't got all day."

"OK. Which bit's mine?"

"Here," I said, pointing. "I've underlined it in red pen. It comes after the verse, which is the most important bit. I'll do that on my own. We'll have a practice-run first. It's essential not to make any mistakes."

"Right," said Alvis, frowning. "The red bits, you say?"

"The red bits. Go on."

"Yeah. Right. OK. Cool. Hey." He cleared his throat. "Ahem. Here goes. *Cur . . . sir . . . Cir-cle of . . . duh . . . eh . . . Dentistry, Circle of . . .*"

"*Destiny*," I corrected him. "I think you'll find that reads *Circle of Destiny*."

"Oh. Yeah, right. It's the funny writing. *Circle of Destiny, Circle of . . . Doop*? Does that say *Doop*?"

"*Doom*," I said tightly. "That's an 'M'. It's a *Circle of Doom*. Does it look like a *Circle of Doop*?"

"Hey. I don't know. You're the expert."

"Yes, well, take my word for it. It's *Doom*."

"OK, I got it . . . *Circle of Destiny, Circle of Doom, Va . . . Varnish this . . .* er *. . . line of dots . . . away fru . . . from this . . . ruh . . . room.*" He looked up brightly. "How was that?"

"Terrible," I sighed. "It's *vanish*, not varnish. We want the wretched mutt to vanish, not come up all shiny. And don't say *line of dots*. That's where you're supposed to insert the name of the thing you want to disappear."

"Oh, I get it. So I say *dog* there, do I?"

"Correct. Try again."

"OK. *Circle of Destiny, Circle of Doom, Vanish this dog away from this room.* That's not right."

"What do you mean, not right?"

"Well, the rhythm of the second bit doesn't work. The dog's all wrong."

"Well, we know that," I said, staring coldly at Kissy-Woo, who was still sitting where she'd been put, happily savaging my cloth to death.

"No, I mean the *word* dog. It needs two beats. Believe me, it'd work better. I know about rhythm."

I stared at him. Come to think of it, hadn't he mentioned something about playing the guitar?

"What do you suggest then?" I asked.

"Well, *doggy* would work."

"This is a Magical Incantation, Alvis," I told him. "*Doggies* don't belong in serious Incantations. Anyway, I'm not sure the rhythm is that important."

"Rhythm's always important," Alvis said firmly. "Ask any drummer. You've gotta get the rhythm right, else it all falls to pieces."

"I don't care. I'm not having *doggy*, it's stupid. Think of something else."

We both stared at Kissy-Woo, hoping for inspiration.

"What about *bulgy-eyed whelp who deserves everything that's coming to her*?" I suggested.

"Nope. Too long. *Bow-wow* would work."

"That's worse than *doggy*!" I cried. "Honestly, I don't know why you're making such a *fuss* about this . . ."

"Hey! I got it! *Hound dog!*" Alvis was jiggling about, clicking his fingers. "That'd work. *Vanish this hound dog away from this room. Yeah!*"

"All right," I sighed. "Have it your own way. I've seen *cushions* that would make better hound dogs, but if it makes you happy, we'll use it."

"Cool. Shall I try it again?"

"In a minute. I've got to do one last thing."

I took a flask of yellow liquid from a shelf and uncorked it.

"What's that?" inquired Alvis with curiosity.

"Yellow Lizard Venom. It's standard stuff. Always used in Vanishing Spells."

He looked suitably impressed. I walked slowly around the chalked circle, dripping the venom as I went. Wherever it fell, there was a hissing noise and acrid, yellowish puffs of smoke arose. It was all very Magical and extremely smelly. Kissy-Woo stopped attempting to kill the cloth and looked up uncertainly. Her bulgy eyes sought out Alvis and she gave an anxious little whimper.

"There, there," said Alvis soothingly. "Stay there, that's a good girl. You'll be OK. At least, I *think* you will." He looked at me. "She will, won't she?"

"Oh yes," I assured him.

"You sure it doesn't hurt? Being Vanished?"

"Oh no," I lied. "Of course not." I hadn't a clue actually, never having done it.

"Where does she go? When she's Vanished, I mean?" He really seemed concerned.

"To a lovely wood in the sky," I fabricated. "She'll be

able to do all sorts of hound-dog things. Chase rabbits, scratch at her fleas, eat chop bones from – chop bone trees. She'll love it. In fact, we owe it to her to give her this wonderful opportunity. Now. Shall we get on?"

"Well . . ."

"Good. Stand well back from the Circle. I'll recite the verse. Be ready for the chorus when I give the signal. Speak clearly. No hesitations. No doops."

I flung my arms wide and took up a dramatic stance. Then I took a deep breath and began to speak in my most bloodcurdling tones.

*"Flesh and blood and bone and hair!* (I thundered)
*Vanish now into thin air!*
*Sunk from view! Lost to sight*
*In the shadows of the night!"*

Suddenly, the dungeons *changed*. The temperature dropped and shadows began to converge in corners. The echoes of my voice bounced around the walls. Stinky, sulphurous yellow smoke billowed. A thin, grey mist began to form in the Magic Circle. Kissy-Woo had lost interest in the cloth. She sat up and scratched herself uncertainly.

"Go on," I hissed, nudging Alvis. "Do your bit!"

"Yeah, but . . ."

"Do it!"

"OK, OK. *Circle of Destiny, Circle of* . . . look, are you sure about the wood?"

*"Yes!"*

"And she's not going to be stuck there for ever? She's only a little dog. I mean, you can bring her back?"

"Yes! No! I don't know! *Say the words, will you!*"

"All right, all right. Where was I? *Circle of Destiny, Circle of Doom, Vanish this hound dog from out of this* . . . hey, look! She's going *transparent*!"

He was right. The mist had intensified and turned into thick fog, which was boiling up all around Kissy-Woo. At the same time, her fat little body was giving off an eerie green glow and becoming insubstantial. You could see the brickwork on the far wall through it. She was trembling.

*"Say the last word!"* I howled. *"You've got to complete the Rite! Say the word!"*

But Alvis was pushing past me. Before I could stop him, he had stepped into the Magic Circle and snatched Kissy-Woo up in his arms.

"OK, girl," he said gently. "Don't be scared. Alvis is here. Hey! Weirdsville!"

To my horror, the same thing that was happening to Kissy-Woo was happening to Alvis! He was becoming see-through!

"You idiot!" I screeched, running forward and hopping about on the edge. "I'll try to get you out of there, but don't complete the spell! Whatever happens, don't say the word!"

"What – you mean *room*?" said Alvis. The second he uttered it, there was an ear-splitting thunderclap. The shadows fled, the yellow smoke cleared, the mist faded . . .

. . . and the Circle was empty.

Oh dear. What a catastrophe. I had vanished both of them. All that stuff about the lovely wood in the skies was complete invention, of course. I hadn't the foggiest where things went when they vanished. Neither did I have a clue how to bring them back – if, indeed, that was possible.

I stood there, biting my fingernails, wondering what to do. Vanishing Kissy-Woo in order to spite Scarlettine was fair enough, but Vanishing Alvis was another kettle of fish altogether. He'd just got a new job. Vanishing for ever in your first week is hardly going to endear you to your employer. Daddy was very understanding, but there were limits.

There was only one way to put things right. I would have to go after them. I sighed, went to the drawer and ate the last chocolate biscuit to give me strength to start again from scratch.

Good job I had plenty of Lizard Venom.

# 8. FOREST OF THE LOST

Vanishing is not pleasant, I can tell you that for nothing. You can actually feel yourself fading. Before I was halfway through the Incantation, I had the sensation of a chilly draught blowing through my body. I tried pinching myself for an experiment and my ghostly finger and thumb met with nothing between them. To my credit, I managed to stumble through the rest of it, choking at the unpleasant mixture of damp grey fog and stinking yellow smoke that billowed round me. I closed my eyes and waited nervously for the thunderclap, which came right on cue. There was a sickening sensation in the region that once contained my very solid stomach, together with the horrible feeling that I was tumbling through thin air. Then –

Plop! I landed on something hard.

Cautiously, I opened my eyes and found myself lying flat on my back, staring up into a network of branches. It was daylight and birds were singing. After a moment, I sat up and examined myself. Solid again. Well, that was something.

I looked around. I was in a forest, sitting on a grassy patch, slap in the middle of what looked like a Fairy Ring. I'm not familiar with Fairy Rings. In Wicked Queen circles, they're considered rather soppy. I've seen diagrams of them in beginner Magic books, however, and this one fitted the bill. There were mushrooms, red spotty toadstools and wild flowers growing in the shape of a circle, at any rate.

"Anyone else comin'?" said a sour voice behind me.

I leapt to my feet and whirled around. Standing directly behind me, leaning on a pair of long-handled shears, was a Dwarf. He was dressed in a shabby green jerkin and matching tights with holes in both knees. There was a pointy hat on his head. He examined me rudely through a pair of thick glasses, which looked as though they had been made from the bottoms of milk bottles.

"What?" I said.

"You heard. I asked if anyone else was comin'."

"I shouldn't think so."

"Just the lad, the dog and you then."

"Correct. Who might you be?"

"Wee Jamey Jinnikins, the Ring Keeper. I'm officially responsible for managin' the Fairy Rings round these parts." He pointed his shears at the circle in which I sat. "You've ruined that Ring between you. I gets it all nice, mushrooms all spaced out proper an' primroses growin' in tidy little clumps, then you clumsy great lumps come appearin' out of thin air, squashin' all the toadstools. See what your great foot's done to them bluebells?"

"Mmm. Look, how long ago did they arrive exactly?"

"'Ow should I know? Do I look like I earn enough to own a watch?"

I didn't like his tone. But I needed information. "I didn't mean to the *second*," I said. "Just a general idea will do. Five, ten minutes? Ish?"

"Ten, I s'pose," he conceded sulkily. "Any more daft questions?"

"Yes. Where am I?"

"Ain't you the nosy one? I ought to start chargin'. If you must know, this 'ere's known as the Forest of the Lost. 'Tis a Magical Place. It connects with all forests everywhere in a strange an' mystical way. Ho yes. We gets all sorts passin' through 'ere." He lowered his voice mysteriously, as though he were telling ghost stories over a camp fire. Silly little twerp. "'Tis full o' lost souls, flounderin' around, trying to find the way . . ."

"Yes, yes, all right, Jinnikins or whatever your name is, you can save the doom and despair. I know all about Magic. Which way did my friend go?"

"*More* questions? I *will* start chargin'. That way." He pointed vaguely with his shears. "That'll be threepence. Who are you anyway?"

"Her Royal Highness the Princess Wilma, if it's any

of your business." I don't normally pull rank, but there was something about him that got on my nerves.

"Oooh. Royalty, eh?" he smirked, putting on a silly voice. "In that case, it'll be sixpence. You can afford it."

"My mother happens to be Her Gracious Majesty the Queen of the Night," I told him coldly. "She won't take kindly to your insolence."

"Yeah, yeah. So that's your ma, eh? You're the little fat one with the horrible hair. I've heard about your sisters. Very beautiful, by all accounts."

"That depends on your taste," I said nastily. "And your eyesight. It's clear you're lacking in both. Good day."

I stomped off, feeling mightily put out.

"What about the sixpence?" he shouted.

"Get lost," I snarled over my shoulder.

"Look who's talkin'," he retorted. "You're the one who'll get lost, mark my words. This is the Forest of the Lost, remember? They all gets lost in 'ere."

I ignored him. Horrible little man.

There was a vague trail winding through the trees. I hadn't a better idea, so I followed it, hoping it would lead me to Alvis and Kissy-Woo. I walked briskly. They were only ten minutes or so ahead. They couldn't have gone far. I had just rounded the first bend when another voice hailed me.

"Excuse me!" A small boy and girl stood just behind me. The boy looked about eight. The girl was younger, and held on tightly to the boy's hand, staring at me with round eyes. Her thumb was plugged into her mouth and her nose was running. Both had extremely dirty faces and their hair was full of leaves. They looked as though they had spent the night camping out in a ditch.

"Yes?" I said.

"We saw you arrive in the Ring. If you want to find your way back, you'll need to mark a trail," said the boy, rather pompously I thought.

"Why should I get lost if I stick to the path?" I inquired haughtily. I don't like know-alls.

"Paths have a tendency to run out around here," said the boy. "Believe me, I know about these things. We're always getting lost, aren't we, Gret?"

The small, round-eyed girl nodded solemnly.

Actually, he had a good point. The Fairy Ring obviously connected in some mystic way with the Magic Circle back in the dungeons. I wanted to be sure I could find it again.

"What would you suggest?" I inquired.

"Small pebbles," said the boy unhesitatingly. "Don't use bread, the birds'll eat it. Pebbles are best. We should know. We've had to do it often enough, right, Gret?"

The small girl nodded again, thumb still stuck firmly in her mouth.

"You can have mine, if you like," said the boy generously. He rummaged in his pocket and pulled out two handfuls of small, white pebbles. He was really trying to be helpful. Perhaps he wasn't such a bad sort after all.

"Thanks," I said, taking them. "Don't you need them yourself?"

"No. We're not lost any more. We're only a few

minutes away from the hovel. Come on, Gret. Let's go home. *Again.*"

For some reason, he sounded a bit gloomy. He took the girl's hand and they trudged off into the trees. I felt quite curious about them, but I had enough on my plate without getting involved in somebody else's story. I gave them a little wave, then turned and walked on, dropping the pebbles at intervals.

It was quite pleasant in the forest. There was a cool breeze which set the flowers dancing. At one point, a small rabbit scurried across my path. It was nice to be out, alone with nature for once. Well, I *say* that – but in actual fact, the forest seemed quite crowded. At various times, deep in the trees that lined both sides of the path, I noticed a small girl with a red cloak who a wolf appeared to be be stalking; a taller, barefoot girl, with long yellow hair, filling a basket with twigs; a young man in princely clothes who appeared to be hacking his way through a load of brambles; several suspicious-looking old ladies in long cloaks who were more than likely Witches in disguise; some more Dwarfs (singing a jolly song); three bears, and at least four jaunty youths with red spotted bundles on sticks, who were obviously off to seek their fortunes. None of them took the slightest notice of me. They were all involved in their own business and getting on with their lives, so I left them to it.

The thought did occur to me that my long-lost Aunt Maud might well be wandering around here somewhere. After all, she had vanished. But I hadn't a clue what she looked like, so even if I *did* come across her I wouldn't know it. Anyway, it wouldn't do to complicate matters. I was here to find Alvis, not missing aunties.

I rounded a bend and came across yet another girl, sitting on a fallen log by the side of the trail. A soft-eyed fawn was leaning against her, head on her shoulder. She was hugging a baby rabbit and a crowd of blue tits were fluttering around her head. I have to admit that she was pretty. Ebony black hair, snow white skin, blood red lips, that sort of thing. I would have disliked her on sight except that she looked a bit down in the dumps. Well, actually, she was bawling her head off.

The blue tits flew off at my approach and the fawn trotted away into the trees. The rabbit looked a bit anxious, but stayed put.

"Morning," I said. "You haven't by any chance seen a boy and a dog with strange hair, have you?"

"Which has the strange hair?" sniffed the girl. "The boy or the dog?"

"The boy. The dog's wearing a red jacket."

"No. I've seen three little *pigs* in jackets. They were having an argument about house building or something."

"Wrong story. Pigs are no good to me."

"In that case, I can't help you. Sorry."

She pulled a white hanky from her pocket and blew her delicate little nose.

"Lost, are you?" I inquired.

"Not really. I just thought I'd try vanishing for a bit. To see if anyone notices." She sounded bitter.

"Something wrong at home?" I said. I didn't really want to get involved, but I couldn't just walk on and leave her there, could I?

"Everything!" she burst out, raising sodden eyes. "Father's going to be married to *her* with the frilly red dresses and she doesn't like me and I hate her and she's got father wrapped around her little finger and they keep going out to restaurants without me and father doesn't even *notice* me any more and he says I've got to be nice to *her* or I'll have to go to my room and the least they could do is ask me to be a bridesmaid at the wedding but they haven't and I hate her and if it wasn't for my friends the animals I don't know what I'd do."

Something suddenly went *Ping!* in my brain. I knew who this was.

"Snow Plough, I presume?" I asked, sitting next to her.

"Snow White, actually. Er –?"

"And your father would be King Geraldo of Truss?"

"Well – yes. Should I know you?"

"I'm your new wicked stepmother-to-be's sister," I told her. "I suppose that makes me your wicked step-aunty-to-be. Call me Wilma."

She gave a little gasp and clapped her hand to her mouth.

"Don't look so worried," I said cheerfully. "Scarlettine might be my sister, but she's no friend of mine. You can badmouth her as much as you like. I do. Look, *do* stop crying. It really doesn't help."

"I'm sorry," said Snow White, giving a final dab to her eyes and putting her hanky away. "I'm not always this wet. Usually, I'm more of a singing and dancing type. All I want is to be happy. But how can I be when *she's* around, hogging all the attention and spoiling everything?"

"I know what you mean," I said grimly. "She's like that at home too."

"I just hate the way she shows off, don't you?" sniffed Snow White.

"And those awful red dresses," I said, nodding.

"And the way she *preens* in mirrors all the time."

"And keeps tossing her hair around," I agreed. I was enjoying myself.

"Sometimes I think she's got father under a spell."

"Oh, that goes without saying. Basic love potion in his drink, I'd say. She says not, but I know Scarlettine. Go on. What else do you hate about her? Your turn."

"That horrible flashy coach she drives around in. It's so *gaudy*."

"Absolutely! And you can't trust her. Here's a tip. If she ever offers you food, say *no*. The chances are, it's poisoned."

"*Really?*"

"Oh yes. She's known for it. Poisons are her speciality. Your father got a good food taster, has he?"

"Well, yes . . ."

"Up his wages."

"Oh *dear*. I knew she was wicked, but . . . *Poison?*"

"Snow White," I said. "You don't know the half. If you knew what Scarlettine is capable of, you'd run away right now and live with some bears or something."

"But I'd be so lonely. It's frightening in the forest." Her lower lip trembled. I thought she was going to cry again.

"It won't be for ever. She only wants your dad for his money. She'll get tired of him as soon as that runs out. Then you can come home and comfort him in his grief and make him feel *really* rotten."

"Oh, father's money won't run out. He's terribly rich."

"You haven't seen Scarlettine on a shopping spree."

"But supposing she doesn't get tired of him? Then what? I can't camp out for ever."

My mind raced as I thought about this. Meeting Snow White was an unexpected bonus. There must be some way of using her to my own advantage.

"We need to force her hand," I said. "She has to show herself up, so that your father sees her for the wicked creature she is."

"How?" said Snow White.

"I'm thinking, all right? OK. Listen. I haven't sorted out all the details yet, but this is the broad plan. You make her jealous. So jealous that she can't bear having you around. Goaded to breaking point, she threatens you with something unspeakably nasty."

"Like what?" said Snow White, going pale. Well, paler.

"I don't know. Does it matter? The point is, you run away. You have to. You're in fear for your life. Then, after a bit, you turn up safe and well and point the finger of accusation. Easy. What are you looking so worried about? It's a great plan."

"But I don't want to be in fear for my life," objected Snow White. Tears were welling up again. "And how do I make her jealous?"

"I'm thinking, I'm thinking. Getting at her vanity's the obvious way. Perhaps we could have you win some sort of beauty competition. That'd put her nose out of joint. If there's one thing she can't bear, it's a rival in the pretty face department . . ."

Just then, we were interrupted. Leaves crackled, and yet another girl came hesitantly forward from behind a tree. This one looked about nine or ten. She was barefoot and dressed in shabby clothes. Her eyes were red, as though she had been crying. Honestly. The forest was *stiff* with weeping girls.

"Excuse me . . ."

"Yes?" I said, trying not to sigh.

"I don't want to bother you, but I'm looking for my friend," whispered the small girl. "His name is Kay. Have you seen him anywhere? I've been walking so long, and I'm only a *little* girl . . ."

"Well, there's an awful lot of people milling around," I said. I probably sounded impatient, but I had enough on my plate right now. "Where and how did you lose him exactly?"

"A tall lady in white came and took him away." Another little bell went *Ping!* in my head.

"Don't tell me. Attached his toboggan to the back of her sleigh, yes?"

"Well, yes. But how . . .?"

"That'll be Frostia, my other sister. She's the Queen of the Snow. Oh, don't look so scared, I'm not going to *say* anything. Why does everyone assume I'm on *their* side? Look, try the North Pole. I know for a fact she's got him banged up in her palace. I'd wear a scarf if I was you."

"Oh, thank you!" cried the small girl, awash with gratitude.

"Think nothing of it," I said. "Good luck with your quest. I'd give you a hand, but right now I'm a bit tied up with some other business. What's your name, by the way? Just for the record?"

"Little Gerda."

"Tell you what, Gerda. You make a start and I'll check out how you're getting on in my Crystal Ball. If you're having trouble, I'll step in and lend a hand. How's that?"

"Thank you! Thank You! You've been most helpful, er . . .?"

"Wilma," I said. "Run along, now. Remember – go north. I'll catch you later."

Much to my relief, she ran off into the trees. I wasn't sure, but I think she went south. I had a feeling she would need quite a bit of help. But first things first. I had to finish what I had started with Scarlettine before I moved on to Frostia.

"Are *you* a Wicked Queen, Wilma?" inquired Snow White.

"Not quite," I said grimly. "But I'm working on it. It's the Family business. All the girls end up as Wicked Queens."

"But you *can* work Magic?"

"Oh *yes*. I've got my Grade Three. Why?"

"Why can't you just use your powers to prevent the wedding then? It's a lot simpler."

"Sorry, but I'm not *that* good," I admitted. "A wedding's like a runaway cart. Practically impossible to stop. No, I think we should go with you running away and hiding out in the forest. But we won't set the wheels in motion until *after* the wedding. Right now, they're so wrapped up in each other they probably wouldn't even notice you'd gone. Leave it with me and I'll iron out the details and get back to you." I stood up. "Meanwhile, I'd better be getting on. First things first. I've got to see a boy about a dog."

"Goodbye, Wilma."

"Goodbye, Snow White. Cheer up. I'll sort something out."

And I left her there, looking after me forlornly. As I walked along, I began to feel a bit anxious. After all, it was a big forest. All these interruptions meant that I was losing ground. Alvis and Kissy-Woo could be anywhere by now.

I came across them as I rounded the next bend. Alvis was sitting by a little stream. He was throwing a stick for Kissy-Woo, who was bounding in and out of the water, wagging her tail and yapping excitedly. Her red velvet jacket was rather the worse for wear, I noticed.

"*There* you are!" I said rather crossly, striding up to them.

"Hi, Wilma," said Alvis. "I was hoping you'd show up."

"Wouldn't it have made more sense to wait by the

Fairy Ring, don't you think? Rather than go wandering off?"

"What, hang out with that Dwarf geezer?"

He had a point. "Well, you didn't have to go so far."

"Buster needed a walk."

"*Who?*"

"Buster. That's what I call her. No self-respecting hound dog's called Kissy-Woo. Hey, it's interesting around here. Did you see the wolf following that kid in the red cloak?"

"Yep. Did you see the three bears?"

"Nope. I saw three little pigs though. You?"

"Nope. Snow White saw them, but I didn't."

"Snow What?"

"White. I met a girl called Gerda too. Both were crying. It's a long story – well, two stories, in fact, but they're sort of getting jumbled up. I think they'll fit in quite nicely with my quest for revenge though. I'll tell you later. But right now, we've got to be getting back. I'm supposed to be at the lunch party. They'll be wondering where I am."

"OK. Come on, Buster, we're going home."

"We're not taking *her*. She's staying."

"Ah, come on, Wilma. We can't leave her. Can we, Buster?" Kissy-Woo launched herself at him and covered his face with affectionate licks.

"That was the whole point of the exercise, remember? Vanishing the dog. Well, I've done it, despite you mucking things up by getting in the Circle. She stays and that's final."

"Then so do I," said Alvis simply.

I stared at him. I'm not used to insubordination from the staff. Well, Peevish and Mrs Pudding maybe – but not a gardener's boy.

"I helped you get the job, remember?" I reminded him.

"Yeah, thanks. But you can't leave a poor little dog all on her own to fend for herself. How long d'you think she'd last? You saw the wolf. It's not her fault if your sister's trained her all wrong and she never gets the chance to be a proper dog with a proper dog's name. Is it, Buster?"

"Oh, all right!" I snapped. "If you're going to come over all soppy. Come on then. It's the last time I'm going to ask *you* for any help with my spells."

We found our way back to the Fairy Ring without any further incidents. Well, Kissy-Woo rolled in something rather nasty, but that was about it. There was no sign of Snow White, Gerda, or the boy with the stones and the girl with him. Neither were there any maidens with baskets, witches in disguise, singing dwarfs, bush-hacking princes, wolves, bears, pigs or youths with spotted bundles. Perhaps it was their lunchtime too.

Wee Jamey Jinnikins, the Ring-keeping Dwarf, was still there though. He was leaning on his shears in exactly the same position as before. Goodness knows when he got any work done.

"Had enough, have we?" he jeered, as we came through the trees.

"More than enough, thank you."

"Aye. The Forest of the Lost is more than most can handle."

"Nonsense. I handled it just fine. How does this Fairy Ring work? Do I need to recite an Incantation or click my shoes together or what?"

"You mean you don't know?" he said snidely. "I thought you knew all about Magic."

"I do. I just don't happen to have my wand on me. Are you going to tell me or not?"

"Why should I? Comin' 'ere actin' all hoity-toity, squashin' all my toadstools with yer big fat b–"

"Hey," said Alvis softly. "This here is the Princess Wilma you're talking to."

"So?"

"So show a bit of respect, right?"

"Oh yeah? An 'ow you gonna make me?"

"Well, I could set the dog on you, for a start."

"Ha! That little bath mat? Why, I'd soon . . ."

His voice trailed off. Alvis had set Kissy-Woo down. Her hair was bristling and a deep growling was coming from her throat. Stiff-legged, she advanced slowly on the Dwarf, who turned rather pale.

"Let me rephrase that," he said hastily. "There's nothing I'd sooner do than help you good folk. Just stand in the Circle, say *Home, James*, and *pfffff!* you'll be there. Nothing to it."

And that's exactly what we did. It worked too. I must say, I'm rather impressed with Fairy Rings. They're a lot more straightforward than Magic Circles.

# 9. HOME AGAIN

"*Kissy-Woo! There* you are! Where have you been? Just look at the state of you! You're all wet and your lovely new jacket's *ruined*! And – uugh! You *stink*! What have you been doing with her, Wilma, you . . . you . . ."

Scarlettine was so beside herself with fury, she couldn't get the words out. She and Mother stood in the Great Hall. It was empty, apart from Peevish, who was clearing the remains of lunch from the sideboard. Kissy-Woo stood at my side, all wet and muddy and happy, with her tail wagging. Her velvet jacket was split down one side. She smelled terrible.

It was left up to me to make all the explanations. As soon as we had arrived back in the Circle, Alvis had gone rushing off to spray for black fly, leaving me to face the music. Well, I suppose he had been away from his duties for some time. Daddy was a trusting sort of employer, and, quite rightly, he didn't want to take advantage.

"Yes, Wilma," said Mother, in steely tones. "What *have* you been doing? We've been looking everywhere for Kissy-Woo. Poor Scarlettine's been out of her mind with worry. It quite spoiled her day."

"That's right! It did! Tell her, Mother!" raged Scarlettine. "You tell her!"

"I just took her for a walk," I said. "Then she Vanished." Well, it was true.

"How *could* you, Wilma!" said Mother. She was so put out, her Aura was nearly black. "You've quite ruined my lunch party. We all spent so long looking for the dog, the food was quite spoiled. Mrs Pudding's gone all grim and silent on me."

"Sorry," I said. "Is it late, then?"

"It's *five o'clock*. You've been gone for *hours*. All the guests have gone home. It really is too bad of you."

"Frostia's gone?"

"Uncle Bacchus gave her a lift in his coach. Grandma's gone back to brood in the belfry and Daddy's taken poor Lord Loser to hospital. He had a little accident with the garden rake when he was out dragging the ornamental lake for Kissy-Woo. You see what happens as a result of your thoughtlessness?"

"Why did Daddy take him? Couldn't Lady Luck?"

"She's working. She had an important card game. My friends are busy people, Wilma. They don't get a lot of time off, and when they do, they like to relax and enjoy themselves, not go scurrying around looking for missing dogs. As for me, I can hardly keep my eyes open . . . What *is* it, Scarlettine?"

Scarlettine had just given a sharp little scream and was staring in horror at her hand, on which was inscribed a neat little semicircle of teeth marks.

"She bit me!" she gasped. "Kissy-Woo! I think I'm going to faint!"

So saying, she collapsed with a loud thump.

"Oh *dear*!" cried Mother. "*Now* see! Peevish, see to the Queen of Mirrors, would you? She appears to have fainted."

She turned on me with a look of accusation.

"Don't look at me," I said. "*I* didn't do anything."

"*Liar!*" spat Scarlettine, immediately sitting up. "Stop *pulling* at me, Peevish, can't you see I've come round? You've done something to her, Wilma, I know you have. Why would she turn on her own mummy unless you'd done something? She's changed. You've put a hex on her, haven't you? Come on, admit it! Make her admit it, Mother! Make her! Make her!" She leapt up, crimson in the face, and began stamping her foot.

"Now then, darling," said Mother soothingly. "Calm down. You don't want to upset yourself today of all days. Not when you've just become engaged."

"But Kissy-Woo bit me! Look! I've got *marks*!"

"Yes, yes, I know, I *know*."

"My own dog *snapped* at me."

"I know, I know, I *know*."

"But she's never done that before. *Never!*"

"I know, I know, I know, I *know*. It's just the fresh air gone to her head, that's all."

"And she's *filthy*! I can't take her home in the coach like that. She'll get mud all over the upholstery!"

"Well, that's easily sorted out. Leave her here with us and Wilma will give her a lovely bath, won't you, Wilma? Don't make a face, that's the least you can do. So you see, Scarlettine, it's all sorted. You can come and collect her tomorrow when she's all clean. Or, if you're too busy, you can leave her here until you come over next weekend."

What, *again*? She was coming *again*?

"What's happening next weekend?" I inquired.

"Scarlettine's bringing her fiancé to tea," Mother told me rather coldly. "It'll be an informal little engagement party. Just the immediate Family. I hope you don't show us all up again like you did today, Wilma. I'm sure King Geraldo won't be amused by your silly pranks. Now, kindly take the dog along to the kitchen and ask Mrs Pudding to heat up some water. What *have* you let her roll in?"

"I'm not sure," I said, adding truthfully, "but I think it might be bear poo."

"*Bear poo?* In the grounds of the *Ancestral Halls*? I hardly think so, Wilma. Was that supposed to be a joke?"

"You see? She thinks it's *funny*!" howled Scarlettine, claws out. "Let me get at her!"

"Now, now, Scarlettine, that's enough," begged Mother, holding her back. "Wilma, please will you *go*!"

I went, taking Kissy-Woo with me. In the kitchen, Mrs Pudding was standing with her arms folded, overseeing the washing up. A team of terrified maids and kitchen boys were scraping leftovers into the bin and piling crockery on to the draining board.

"Look at it!" snapped Mrs Pudding. "Half of it thrown away. Waste of good food. What is it you want, Miss Wilma?"

"Mother says I have to bath Kissy-Woo," I said humbly. "Can I have some hot water, please?"

"No," said Mrs Pudding. "Get the filthy thing out of my kitchen. She's spooking Denzil."

A low hissing from the top of the dresser confirmed that Denzil was indeed spooked. Kissy-Woo looked up, spotted her, and set up a high-pitched yapping that set everyone's teeth on edge. Denzil retaliated by lashing his tail to and fro and spitting. They don't get on.

"What about some lunch then?" I inquired, not very hopefully.

"Lunch is over. You either eat at the proper time or you don't eat at all. I've got enough to do, what with all this to clear up and your grandma wantin' her sprouts. By the way, there's a message for you from that new gardening boy with the funny hair. He says he's off duty and he'd like a word."

"Really? Where is he?"

"In his room, I suppose."

"But I thought he lived in a caravan."

"Eh? No, he's moved into the servants' quarters. Orders of the King. Out the door, along the corridor, down the steps, third door on the right."

I had no idea that Alvis was living in. Come to think of it, I didn't know very much about him at all.

I followed Mrs Pudding's instructions and found the third door on the right. From inside came the muted sounds of strumming. I knocked. The sounds stopped and a moment later the door opened.

"Hey," said Alvis. "Come on in."

He was wearing the strange outfit he had on the first time I saw him. The huge spangly jacket and the narrow trousers and the thick-soled blue shoes. His greasy lock of hair hung before one eye, as usual. In his hand, he held a guitar.

I had never seen a guitar before. We're not a very musical Family. There is a huge organ in one of the rooms, but I've never seen anyone play it. There's a rumour that Grandma used to play it once, but not any more. She doesn't do anything since she retired into her permanent sulk. Uncle Bacchus threatens us with a nose harp every so often and is always telling us he had trumpet lessons when he was a boy, but we don't encourage him.

Alvis's guitar was rather special, I could see that. It had been lovingly polished and was brown as a new conker.

Kissy-Woo jumped up, wagging her tail in ecstatic greeting, then began to sniff around his room. I walked in and looked around with great curiosity. It was very bare. Just a bed, a cupboard, a small table containing a big jar of hair grease, a wash bowl and a small mirror. That was it. No family photographs. No personal bits and bobs, apart from the hair grease.

"Hmm. So this is your room. It's very *basic*, isn't it?"

"I guess so. I travel light." Alvis removed Kissy-Woo

from the bed and placed her firmly on the floor. "Stay there, Buster." She obediently lay down and laid her head on her paws.

"How come you can make her do things when nobody else can?" I asked.

"I dunno. I guess I take after Ma."

"What does your ma *do*, Alvis?"

"This and that. Hey, that was some weird stuff that happened, eh? What about that forest? That was some place, right? Who were those weeping girls you were going to tell me about?"

I had a feeling he was trying to change the subject. I decided to go along with him. It doesn't pay to push things. Sooner or later I'd find out.

I sat on the edge of the bed and explained about the whole business of Scarlettine's engagement and Frostia's kidnapped boy and where Snow White and Gerda fitted in. While I talked, he picked up his guitar and began to quietly pluck the strings. He was good. I could tell.

". . . so that's how it was left," I finished, at the end of the long, complicated story. "I more or less promised to help both of them. And helping *them* fits in rather neatly with my own plans, don't you see?"

"Right. Good thing you came across them, eh?"

"Yes. Lady Luck must have been on my side, for once." Actually, she couldn't have been. She was on her way to a card game at the time, leaving her poor little husband to fall in the lake.

"So what happens next?" asked Alvis. "Any ideas?"

"Loads," I said airily. "It's just a matter of deciding the best one."

Actually, I was still hazy on the details. But I wasn't going to admit it. It had been a busy old day and I was feeling rather tired. Best to sleep on it and hope for inspiration.

I stood up, yawning, and announced my intention of going to bed. Alvis very kindly offered to deal with bathing Kissy-Woo, then played me a little tune on his guitar. It was rather nice actually.

He's odd. But I do like him.

# 10. THE ENGAGEMENT PARTY

"More *home-made* tomato soup, King Geraldo?" asked Mother. "There's plenty in the pot. Peevish, serve His Majesty with more *home-made* tomato soup. The tomatoes come from our own garden. My husband grows them, you know. I do so love *home-made* tomato soup. Such a lovely shade of green, I always think."

She patted Daddy's hand proudly. He looked pleased. They do get on well, even though they're so different.

"No, thank you," said King Geraldo, hastily covering his soup bowl with heavily be-ringed, podgy little hands. "I have a stomach condition. I have to be careful. Heh, heh, heh, heh, heh."

"Poor Gerry," cooed Scarlettine. "He's so delicate. The slightest little thing upsets his tum-tum, doesn't it, darling?"

I didn't much like King Geraldo. He was a short, plump little man with watery eyes, and he wore purple knickerbockers. Snow White certainly didn't inherit her good looks from him. You could tell he was ridiculously rich though. His tall crown was studded with fist-sized diamonds and he dripped with rings, medals and medallions. He had a silly little laugh too. *Heh, heh, heh, heh, heh.* It really got on your nerves.

We all sat around the long table drinking green tomato soup (apart from Grandma, who was silently shovelling down her usual sprouts) and making forced conversation. Mother, anxious that Geraldo get a good impression of us, had made Uncle Bacchus wear a suit. She had also confiscated his secret bottle. He wasn't himself at all.

Frostia was in a mood, I could tell. She had tried to whip up a bit of interest in her kidnapped boy, but everybody's eyes were on Scarlettine and Geraldo. They sat next to each other, holding hands. Scarlettine kept batting her eyes at him and pretending to pick bits of fluff from his shoulders. He was completely besotted with her. When nobody was looking, he kept blowing her little kisses. It was quite sickening.

"So, Geraldo, old boy," said Daddy, "have you decided when the wedding is to be?"

"Heh, heh, heh, heh, heh. Well . . ."

"Quite soon," chipped in Scarlettine. "I thought next month."

"Next *month*?" cried Mother. "Oh my! I shall have to ring my dressmaker *immediately*! Did you hear that, Mama? Our baby's getting married next month!"

"These sprouts is hard again," said Grandma darkly. "I keep tellin' her, but it don't make no difference."

There was an awkward little pause. Most people were familiar with Grandma's little ways, but Geraldo was a newcomer.

"Sprouts, eh?" said King Geraldo. "Fond of them, are you, ma'am?"

You could cut the tension with a knife. Nobody ever remarks on Grandma's strange diet. It's just not done. She looked up very slowly from her plate, fixed her hooded eyes on him and reached for her stick, which lay on the floor next to her chair.

"Who's this?" she hissed.

"Now then, Mama," said Mother hastily. "This is King Geraldo, Scarlettine's fiancé. Peevish, take the Queen Mother's stick and put it somewhere safe before somebody trips over it." She turned brightly to King Geraldo, who was looking rather bewildered. "Scarlettine tells me you have a lovely palace. *Do* tell us all about it."

"Ah. Well . . ."

"It's full of priceless antiques, isn't it, Gerry?" interrupted Scarlettine. "He collects them, you know. He has some wonderful mirrors, don't you, darling? That's what we have in common. Our love of mirrors. That's how we met. In an auction room. We were both bidding for a lovely little diamond-backed looking-glass, remember, darling? And do you know what he did? He bought it for me, the sweet, sweet pet." She leaned over and planted a kiss on his cheek.

"Heh, heh, heh," tittered King Geraldo, gazing at her like a sick puppy.

"Aaah," cooed Mother. "Look at them, George. Such lovebirds."

"Mmm," said Daddy, pushing his soup bowl away. Like me, I think he was beginning to feel a little sick. "I hear you have a daughter, old chap."

"Ah, yes. My little Snow White." King Geraldo came over all sentimental. "Happy as the day is long. Always singing and dancing, pretty as a picture . . ."

"Prettier than me?" inquired Scarlettine sharply, sticking out her lower lip. We were getting into dangerous waters.

"Oh no, my love. Of course not, just different."

"Do go on, Geraldo," urged Daddy, with a cross look at Scarlettine.

"Eh? Oh. Ah. My Snow White. Hair as black as ebony . . ."

"Of course, there's *loads* to do before the wedding," butted in Scarlettine defiantly. "I thought I'd ask Mrs Pudding to make the cake. And then there's my dress. I want a long, long train. I shall need at least six pageboys to carry it."

"You'd better not wear white," put in Frostia, sounding crabby. "I'm wearing white. It's my colour."

"If I wanted to, I would. It's my wedding and I can wear what I like. But I shan't. I shall wear red. Geraldo loves me in red, don't you, darling?"

"Eh? Oh yes, my love. Red as a rose, eh? Heh, heh, heh."

"I shall wear sky blue," murmured Mother. Eyebrows went up. She *always* wears black. "Well, I'm not going to be on duty on my own daughter's wedding day, am I? We want the sun to shine. Black suits me better, of course, but we must all make sacrifices."

"You were telling us about your daughter," Daddy reminded King Geraldo. "Do go on, old boy."

"Yes. Well, she's got hair as bla –"

"And then, of course, there are all the invitations to make out!" cried Scarlettine, never one to back down. "I do want a lovely, *big* wedding! I can, can't I, Gerry? No expense spared, that's what you said."

"Oh – er – yes, dearest, whatever you like."

"You see? He's *soooo sweeeet*."

"Where would we be without our lovely daughters, eh?" persisted Daddy. "I must admit I'm surprised you didn't bring little Snow White along today to meet us all."

"Well, I would have, but . . ."

". . . she's out playing with her little animal friends," Scarlettine finished off for him. "Isn't that right, Gerry? I *did* ask her, but she didn't want to come. I think she's a teeny-weeny bit jealous of me." She gave a sad little sigh. "Oh well. I'm sure she'll learn to love me in time. Everyone does."

This was just *too* much. Frostia certainly couldn't take it. She set down her glass of iced milk with an irritable click. "I think I should be off soon, Mother. I have the boy to feed."

"Oh, not *yet*, darling. We haven't even had the main course. Mrs Pudding would be terribly upset. She's made a special effort. And there's ice cream for pudding. Your favourite."

"Fond of animals, is she, Snow White?" inquired Daddy. For once, he had really got the bit between his teeth.

"Oh, yes. Why, she . . ."

"The trouble *is*," interrupted Scarlettine, "the trouble *is*, poor Gerry's allergic to the *hair*, you see. It's all very well Snow White traipsing around the place with all those deer and rabbits in tow, but it brings on the sneezums, doesn't it, popsicle?"

"Yes," admitted King Geraldo. "Heh, heh, heh. I'm rather afraid it does."

"So I've told her she has to keep them outside from now on. 'Snow White,' I said. 'I *know* you love your animals, but don't you think it's just a teensy-weensy bit *selfish*, when your father's got such trouble with his sinuses?' She tried to argue, but I had to be firm, I'm afraid. I'm only thinking of you, darling. You know that." She leaned towards him and dropped a kiss on his ear.

I decided to stick my oar in. It seemed as good a time as any.

"So what's going to happen to Kissy-Woo?" I asked. "Won't she bring on the sneezums?"

"Oh, *Kissy-Woo*! Huh. I'm not having *her* back after last weekend," sniffed Scarlettine. "Who needs her? You can keep her here or give her away to a dogs' home."

Even Mother looked surprised at this.

"*Really*, Scarlettine? But Wilma gave her a bath and everything. You don't want her back?"

"Oh, I *adored* her, of course, but we all have to make sacrifices in the name of love. I just wish I could get Snow White to see that." Scarlettine heaved a little sigh.

Honestly. What a snake she is. Mind you, as far as Kissy-Woo was concerned, it was all for the best. Alvis had taken her under his wing, and I had to admit she was becoming quite bearable. I was even beginning to think of her as Buster.

Just then, Mrs Pudding stuck her head around the door and inquired whether the soup was all right. I noticed Denzil twining around her ankles. He's not allowed in the dining room, particularly when he's moulting. I made encouraging little noises and he came running over and jumped delightedly on my lap. Nobody noticed. They were all too busy making grovelling soup-praising noises. I put a napkin over him and tried not to wince as he started rhythmically sinking his claws in and out of my leg.

Mrs Pudding began loading empty soup plates on to her tray. She paused when she got to King Geraldo and looked pointedly at his bowl. It was brimful of soup which he obviously hadn't touched.

"Something wrong with it?" she asked grimly.

"I beg your pardon?" said King Geraldo.

"My soup. Something wrong with it?"

"Oh – er – no, no. Heh, heh, heh."

Mrs Pudding is touchy about her cooking. She takes it personally if you don't have a clean plate. King Geraldo's plate was insultingly full.

"It's good soup, that is."

"Madam, I'm sure it is, it's just that I have a – *achoo*!- excuse me – a – *achoo*!" King Geraldo fished out a handkerchief and mopped at his nose. On my lap, beneath the napkin, Denzil purred hysterically and dribbled on my knees. I tickled him beneath the chin.

"His Majesty has a delicate stomach, Mrs Pudding," Mother hastened to explain. "He was only just telling us all about it, weren't you, King Geraldo?"

"Yes, I – *achooooo*! I'm afraid I – *aaa . . . aaaaa . . .*"

"Nasty cold you've got there, old chap," observed Daddy.

". . . *choo*! Bit of an *aaa . . . aaaa . . . aller . . . choo*! Allergy." He wiped his streaming eyes.

"Poor *darling*!" cried Scarlettine, all false, fluttering concern. "You've got the *sneezums* again. Whatever can have brought it on? It's not as if there are any animals in here."

"Not my soup, that's for sure," snapped Mrs Pudding. "He hasn't touched a drop, look. Perfectly good soup, gone to waste. If he doesn't want it, why stick it in his bowl, that's what I'd like to know."

"*Scarlettine!*" trilled Mother, a touch desperately. "Why don't you show Uncle Bacchus your lovely engagement ring? I don't think he's had a proper look at it yet. You'd like to see Scarlettine's ring, wouldn't you, Bacchus?"

"Eh?" Uncle Bacchus jerked awake from the little snooze he was enjoying. His hand went automatically for his secret bottle, which wasn't there.

"Of course you would! Pass it down the table, Scarlettine, Uncle's dying to see."

Thrilled to be the centre of attention again, Scarlettine removed her ring and held it out to Peevish.

"Here, Peevish. Take this to Uncle."

"Certainly, Miss Scarlettine." Peevish reached out to take the ring. At exactly the same moment, King Geraldo let out the sneeze of all sneezes.

"*Rrrrraaaachooooo!*"

It shot out like an express train from a tunnel. His whole body jerked forward and his crown collided with Peevish's hand. The ring flipped from Peevish's fingers, sailed through the air and fell with a little splash into the soup tureen. Scarlettine let out a shrill shriek of dismay. Then, quite beside herself with fury, she turned on King Geraldo with a snarl.

"Idiot! Stupid, careless idiot! Why don't you . . ."

"Scarlettine!" rapped Mother warningly. "Control yourself!"

King Geraldo came out of his hanky and stared at his beloved with horrified eyes. It was obviously the first time he had seen her show her true colours. A silence fell over the table. All eyes were on Scarlettine as she struggled to contain herself.

"W-what?" stammered King Geraldo. "What did you just say?"

Uncle Bacchus saved the day. He lurched to his feet, reached across the table and plunged his hand into the tureen.

"Don't you worry, niece! I'll fish it out," he roared heroically, rooting around. "Don't you fret, it's in here somewhere."

Scarlettine, meanwhile, had recovered her self-control. She forced a bright little smile on her lips and turned to Geraldo.

"I was just saying what a stupid, careless girl I am, letting my lovely ring fall in the soup like that. Oh, darling!" She gave a little gasp. "You didn't think I meant *you*?"

"Well, for a moment there, it rather seemed . . ."

"Here we are!" Uncle Bacchus withdrew his green, dripping hand and held it up triumphantly, like a conjuror. "Eureka! Or should I say – your ring-a!"

Mother and Daddy gave him a little round of applause – rather too soon, as it happened, because the next thing we knew, the ring slipped from Uncle's slimy grasp, fell to the floor and went rolling away across the polished boards. Under the napkin, Denzil stopped purring and became stiff and tense. Then, suddenly, he shot from my lap and went racing off after the ring. It was an interesting, if unexpected, development.

"It's Denzil!" screamed Scarlettine, springing to her feet. "Wilma's had the wretched animal in here all along! No wonder Geraldo's been sneezing! Stop him, someone! He's hunting my *ring*!"

He was too. There's something about a small, moving, circular object that brings out the kitten in all cats, and Denzil was no exception. He caught up with the ring in seconds, bringing his paw down and stopping it in its track. He crouched over it, tail swishing. He backed off, wiggling his rear end, eyeing it as though it were a cornered mouse. Then, to the horror of everyone present – except me, it must be confessed – he sprang on it! His long, pink tongue came out and swept it into his mouth. He swallowed, choked, swallowed again, gave one solitary hiccup, then sat back and proceeded to wash his whiskers.

Scarlettine let out a banshee wail, shot from her seat, raced across the hall – and was on him! She picked him up by his tail and shook him like a pepper pot. Denzil let out a howl of protest, lashed out with his back legs and scratched her from elbow to wrist. Scarlettine screamed again and carried on shaking.

"Scarlettine!" Mother was on her feet now and hastening across the hall. "You're out of control! Put the cat down! Look at you, you're bleeding like a stuck pig! Bacchus! Bring a cloth or something to bind around her arm!"

Uncle Bacchus never does things by degrees. With a grand gesture, he took hold of the tablecloth and gave a mighty pull. Knives, forks, bread rolls and soup tureen went crashing to the floor. Everyone leapt up in a panic. Chairs were overturned. King Geraldo's foot skidded in a puddle of soup. He staggered, clutched at Frostia in order to save himself and then they both went down with sad little cries. Frostia lay outstretched in a froth of green soup-stained petticoats. Geraldo's little purple legs wiggled in the air. I thought I'd die from suppressed laughter.

All was pandemonium. Grandma was scuttling around looking for her stick, intent on zapping someone. Peevish was ringing his hands and quietly moaning. Uncle Bacchus went striding up to Scarlettine, trailing the tablecloth in his wake, intent on using it as some sort of giant bandage. Daddy was patting her soothingly on the back and attempting to prise Denzil from her fist. Mother's Aura had gone so black that you couldn't see her. And Mrs Pudding? I'll tell you what she did. She marched over to Scarlettine, mouth set in a grim line.

"Don't you do that to my Denzil, Miss Scarlettine!" she snapped. "I'll give you what for, you naughty!"

And she smacked her sharply on the wrist! Scarlettine's hand opened and Denzil dropped to the floor and fled from the hall with a yowl.

I will draw a veil over the rest of the proceedings. Suffice to say that the engagement party was not a success. I was banished to my room, where I sat by the window and watched Frostia depart in her sleigh in high dudgeon, shortly followed by King Geraldo (still sneezing and looking rather put out, as anyone would be who had just had a priceless ruby eaten by a cat) and Scarlettine, weeping copiously and with her arm wrapped in the tablecloth. They climbed into Geraldo's coach and took off in a cloud of dust. Neither bothered to wave.

I got a strong telling-off that evening. The general feeling was that it was all my fault. Well, I suppose it was. I felt a bit rotten about poor Denzil's rough treatment, particularly as he didn't appear for his supper that night. Tummy ache, I suppose. But the following morning, after a visit to his soil patch, he came bouncing in through the kitchen window, purring and demanding his breakfast.

What became of the ring? I'll leave it to your imagination.

# 11. THE MAGIC MIRROR

It takes more than an eaten engagement ring and an unsuccessful party to stop a wedding. I realized that when Mother summoned me into her chamber and demanded to know what I intended to buy Scarlettine and Geraldo for their wedding present.

"Oh," I said. "It's going ahead then, is it?"

"Of course it's going ahead. Scarlettine tells me Geraldo has bought her an even bigger ring. He loves her more than ever, no thanks to you." Mother's bed was heaped with new blue gowns and she was trying on various hats. "He's been very gracious about it all, despite you showing the Family up in a bad light. I don't know what you were thinking of, Wilma. Sneaking the wretched cat in and bringing on the poor man's allergy."

"I didn't sneak him in."

"Enough! I don't want to hear any more about it. The very least you can do is make amends by buying them a decent wedding present. And I mean *decent*. I shall want to know what it is, so don't think you can get away with any old rubbish."

"But I don't have any money!" I wailed. "I spent it all on supplies from the catalogue. You told me I was to take Magic seriously. You said you wanted me to take my Grade *Four*."

"I'm not interested in your excuses. Anyway, you spend too much time down in that lab of yours. Don't think I don't know about the chocolate biscuits you've got down there. I don't think you do any serious studying at all. You'll just have to earn some money by doing jobs around the place. I'm sure Mrs Pudding or Peevish can find you something to do. Or you can help Daddy in the garden."

"*Jobs?*" I cried. "But I'm a Princess! Royalty don't do *jobs*!"

"Nonsense. *I* have a job. So do your sisters. It'll be good practice for when you become a Queen. *If* you ever make Queen, that is." She gave a sigh. "Sometimes I wonder."

"But –"

"Go. Before I lose my temper."

Fuming, I turned on my heel and stomped out. *Jobs* indeed. The last thing I intended to do was a load of jobs in order to buy rotten old Scarlettine a rotten old present. She's never bothered to buy me one, after all. But Mother had made it very clear that a present was expected.

Mournfully, I wandered through the palace. I wondered whether to call into the kitchen, but decided against it. Mrs Pudding was having a massive cupboard clear-out. I could hear her shouting at her weeping troops several corridors away. I tapped on Alvis's door, but there was no reply. I guessed he was out working somewhere in the grounds. Come to think of it, Daddy had remarked that they were expecting a delivery of mulch. Whatever that was, I didn't like the sound of it. It rather seemed as though I was on my own.

I debated whether to go down to my lab and take a look in my Crystal Ball. Seeing Frostia had reminded me that I really should check to see how Gerda was getting on with her quest. Badly, I suspected. Frostia certainly hadn't mentioned any rescue attempt, so I guessed the poor little thing was still shivering under a bush somewhere on her way to the North Pole. On the other hand, I was still far from getting my revenge on Scarlettine. Perhaps I should be concentrating on that, seeing as the wedding was imminent. It was all so complicated with the two of them.

My wanderings had brought me to the foot of the narrow, winding staircase which led to the attic. A thought suddenly struck me. There was all kinds of junk up there. Maybe something suitable for a wedding present! I could dredge up some old thing, dust it off and make out I had bought it from an antique shop. Good thinking!

I began to climb. It was ages since I had visited the attic. I had forgotten how long the staircase was. I stopped halfway up to catch my breath by a little window, rubbed away a patch of dust and looked out. I saw the sky – dark and lowering because Mother was awake – and the palace roofs. Far away, in the distance, I spotted Daddy and Alvis standing by a pile of steaming brown stuff. Mulch, probably. Kissy-Woo, free from the tyranny of Scarlettine's lap, was rushing about snapping at pigeons and having the time of her life.

I looked the other way, towards the belfry. I noticed that the curtains were firmly drawn. Grandma had shut herself in after the engagement party and was refusing to come out. She wouldn't even allow anyone in with her sprouts. They had to knock three times and leave them outside the door. Her sulk was deeper and darker than ever before. Aunt Maud had a lot to answer for.

Having recovered a bit of puff, I went on up the stairs. At the very top, there was a small, wooden door. The hinges squealed as I pushed it open. Nobody had been up here for a very long time. I could tell that from the huge spider's web that hung across the black entrance. I brushed it away and stepped in. The last time I ventured up here, I came across a highly unpleasant old woman sitting at an ancient spinning wheel. "Wrong palace," I told her sharply. "Clear off." She muttered something about only having to look at me to know that I was the wrong princess and vanished in a puff of smoke. There was no sign of her today, however.

I fumbled for the candle stub and matches which were kept on a ledge just inside the door. We don't use Magic candles in the attic. No point when nobody ever comes up here. I lit the candle and held it aloft. As well as the glass slippers, the seven-league boots, the broomsticks and the cauldrons, which I think I mentioned earlier, there were old brass-bound chests, a mangle, boxes of mouldering wrapping paper, a tailor's dummy, a telescope, a wardrobe, tins of paint, rolls of wallpaper, teetering piles of ancient magazines, boxes of chipped china, an old treadle sewing machine, a wind-up gramophone, a full suit of rusty armour, a parrot cage, a stack of old oil paintings, a butterfly net, a rabbit hutch and a printing press. That was just for starters. Like the dungeons, the attic goes on for ever. I've never dared explore beyond the area just inside the door. I've a feeling that if you went too far, you would never find your way back again.

Wrinkling my nose at the musty smell, I moved further in. I ignored the stuff I've just mentioned. There was nothing there that would do as a wedding present. Scarlettine would probably recognize it anyway. We were banned from the attic as small children, but I know for a fact that she and Frostia used to hide just inside the door and have a lot of girlish fun hacking up my dollies.

The further in I walked, the darker it became. I turned a corner and began edging sideways down a narrow alley with walls of tightly packed pieces of forgotten furniture: a mad jumble of mouldering sofas, upside down tables and rotting chests of drawers. Every step I took raised a cloud of dust.

I reached a place where the alley branched off into two. One path was formed by banks of crumbling cardboard boxes and tottering piles of old gardening magazines. The walls of the other consisted of piles of huge copper kettles on one side and a snarl of old hatstands on the other. Nothing here of any use.

I was beginning to feel nervous being so far away from the door. Perhaps further exploration wasn't such a good idea. I turned to retrace my steps – and got a rather nasty shock. There, at the very end of the left-hand alley, was a glowing, ghostly face! It hovered a few feet from the floor. I could make out hollow eyes, a flaring nose, a jutting chin and . . .

. . . horrible hair. Lank and greasy, like mice tails in butter. I knew that hair when I saw it. Yes, folks, it was me! I was looking at myself in a mirror! I let out a huge sigh of relief, chuckled a bit, more for the comfort of hearing my own voice than anything, and was just about to retrace my steps when a thought struck me.

A mirror! Of *course*! What could be better than a mirror for a wedding present? It was perfect. Scarlettine was the Queen of Mirrors, Geraldo liked antiques, it might just fit Mother's definition of a decent present and I wouldn't have to cough up a penny. Fingers crossed it wasn't cracked . . .

Eagerly I set off down the alley. As I neared the mirror, I felt even more encouraged. It was oval-shaped and set on a carved mahogany stand. I stopped before it and, using the edge of my sleeve, gave the dusty surface a brisk rub.

A funny thing happened then. Instead of my candlelit reflection becoming clearer, the glass instantly darkened until I couldn't see myself at all. Hastily, I snatched my hand away. Grey mists swirled about. Strange shapes formed, broke up and then re-formed into even stranger ones. Then, suddenly, there was a Face.

Not my face. I'm no oil painting, as I'm the first to admit, but compared to *this* Face, I was a raving beauty. *This* Face was long and bad-tempered-looking, with a definite green tinge. By the expression, I had a feeling it had just woken up. The nose was big and bulbous, with a ring through it. The head was a shaved dome between two large, curved horns. There was no body attached. Just the Face, floating there in a sea of swirling mist, glaring out at me through yellow, bleary eyes.

We looked at one another, the Face and I. Then it spoke.

"Get on with it then," it said. I had expected deep, booming tones, but in fact the voice that issued forth was flat, with an irritable edge to it.

"Get on with what?" I inquired.

"What d'you think? The *Quethtion*, of courthe." Oh dear. It had a lisp too.

"What question?"

The Face gave a sigh and rolled its eyes upwards.

"Give me thtrength," it muttered, then wearily lowered its gaze to stare at me again. "Don't tell me. You haven't read the *inthtructionth*, have you?"

"What instructions?"

"Tch, tch," tutted the Face. "What *ith* it with you girlth? Look down on the pedethtal. There'th a brath plaque. There. No, not there! To the left! There! Thee?"

I bent down, stuck my candle in a notch in the floorboards and went to work with the hem of my dress. Sure enough, beneath the thick layer of dust, I found a small, square strip of metal with a raised pattern bearing the universally recognized Magical symbol of the lightning bolt.

"Got it."

"About time. Preth it, then. *Preth* it!"

Gingerly, I placed my thumb on the plaque and pushed. When I released the pressure, it sprang upwards on a hinge, revealing a tiny cavity beneath which held a small piece of yellowing paper.

"What's this?" I asked.

"The *inthructionth*!" shrieked the Face, really quite agitated. "What d'you think? Now, why don't you try *readin' 'em*? I take it you *can* read?"

"Certainly I can read," I snapped. I turned my back on him and carefully unfolded the paper. There were several lines of faded writing in a flowing script. I brought the candle close and studied them. This is what I read:

*Congratulations! Thou art now the proude owner of Ye Genuine Magick Mirror! Features include:*

- ✘ *Strong supporting frame*
- ✘ *Cunninge secrete compartement*
- ✘ *Exceptional rhyming performance*

*from Ogggg, thy very own personalized Trapped Spirite*

*Warning*

*Ogggg can be touchy. To prevent insult hazard, ask thou the following question Only:*

*Mirror, mirror on the wall,*

*Who is the fairest of them all?*

*Enjoy!*

Honestly! What a load of fuss over a silly old looking-glass which only had the one function.

"Is that all you do then, Ogggg?" I sneered, folding up the paper and turning back to the Face. "Answer the one question?"

"That'th it," he snapped. "Jutht the one."

"So basically, correct me if I'm wrong, you are a trapped spirit employed as some sort of glorified beauty consultant?"

"Yeth. Athk the quethtion."

"Have you looked at yourself lately? You're hardly qualified to judge beauty, are you? It's like asking a warthog to judge the Cutest Fluffy Chick Competition. What makes you such an expert?"

"Look," said Ogggg, eyes glittering malevolently, "*are* you going to athk the quethtion or aren't you?"

"No," I said. "I wouldn't give you the satisfaction."

There was a little pause.

"Go on," said Ogggg. "I'm here now. You might ath well."

"No. You just want an excuse to be rude."

"Oh, go *on*. Be a thport. I do it in poetry, you know. I've been told I'm rather good." His voice had taken on an unpleasant, wheedling tone.

"Shush. I'm thinking."

I paced up and down a bit. The candle was dripping wax on my fingers and I thought I saw a spider. Grade Three Magic or not, I'm not keen on spiders. I wanted to speed things up a bit. And suddenly, in a flash of inspiration, I had it. I knew *exactly* how to get my revenge on Scarlettine.

"Look, Ogggg," I said, "I want to be quite straightforward with you. I take it you're not happy in your work?"

"What do you think? How would you like to be thtuck behind a sheet of flyblown glath for hundredth of yearth anthering daft quethtionth about who'th fair and who ithn't? Ath if I cared."

"As I thought. Now, listen. I have a proposal."

And, as briefly as I could, I gave him the background. I painted a brief, unflattering portrait of Scarlettine, emphasizing how vain she was. I told him about her forthcoming marriage to Geraldo. I mentioned my meeting with Snow White. I told him of my plan to get revenge. Through it all, he listened unblinkingly – although I think I noticed a tear in his eye when I went on about poor, innocent little Snow

White, whose dear father was under the spell of my scheming sister. I laid that bit on with a trowel.

"Tho?" he said, when I had finished. "What'th the propothal?"

"Here it is, in a nutshell. I give you to Scarlettine as a wedding present. You tell her she's the fairest one of all. You keep telling her that, to lull her into a false sense of security. Then, when she's least expecting it . . . bam! You change your mind. You spring Snow White on her. Mad with jealousy, she tries to get rid of Snow White."

"How do you know that?"

"Believe me, she will. So, Snow White runs away to the forest and lives in a cave with some bears, biding her time until King Geraldo learns the truth. Scarlettine gets booted out, Snow White returns home to her guilt-stricken father, Scarlettine's furious, I get my revenge. How's that for a master plan?"

Ogggg gave it some thought.

"I don't like the bearth," he said, after a bit.

"Bears, pigs, whatever. She's a nice little thing. I'm sure someone will put her up for a bit."

"And what do I get out of thith?"

"Freedom," I said simply. "I don't want to boast, but I'm no slouch in the old Magic department. I'll release you. There's nothing to it. I've done it before."

I had too. I released a Genie from a Lamp for my Grade Three Practical. Releasing Trapped Spirits is a doddle. Anyone who dabbles in the Magic Arts can do it. A couple of mystic signs, a chanted line or two and it's done. If you can't be bothered using Magic, a large brick works just as well. Destroying the thing they're trapped in is the secret. The thing is, nobody wants to. Trapped Spirits are always such miserable so-and-so's and deserve everything they get.

"I'm thuppothed to tell the truth," fretted Ogggg. "It'th what I do. I anther the quethtion truthfully. In rhyme."

"But you *will* be telling the truth, in the end. Snow White *is* the fairest of them all."

"Then I should thay tho to begin with."

I was getting rather tired now.

"Look," I said, "either you play it my way or I leave you up here for another thousand years. Take your pick."

Ogggg considered. Then: "You promith to let me out?"

"I promise. Do we have a deal?"

Slowly, he nodded. It rather seemed that we did.

## 12. HELPING GERDA

It was the following morning. I waited until the sun came out, which meant that Mother was safely asleep. I found Alvis clipping the grass around the base of the belfry. It badly needed doing. Grandma had recently taken to pouring buckets of water on the heads of anyone who came too close and none of the gardeners would go near the place. Kissy-Woo was jumping around behind him, enjoying the great outdoors and looking like she'd never sat on a lap or worn a ribbon in her life. Denzil sat on the branch of a nearby tree. A couple of wood pigeons strolled around Alvis's boots, looking for worms.

"I'm surprised you don't have a loads of blue tits fluttering around your shoulders," I remarked as I walked up. "Snow White does."

"That'd be overkill." Alvis gave me a little grin. "Hi, Wilma." High above us, a curtain twitched. I had the strong feeling that Grandma was watching.

"You're brave," I said, glancing meaningfully upwards. "Most people are soaked by now. I think Grandma lies in wait for the sound of the shears. She's going through one of her bad phases."

"She's OK," said Alvis, straightening up. "Just a bit lonely, I reckon. Mr Peevish asked if I'd take her sprouts up yesterday. Cool bats she's got up there."

"You went *up*? And she didn't threaten to zap you?"

I was amazed. Even Peevish took his life in his hands on the daily sprout delivery. Grandma made it very clear that she Wanted To Be Alone. She really was out of humour these days. Mother was getting quite worried about her. Sulking is one thing, but shutting yourself into a belfry and refusing to communicate with anything other than bats is another. Mind you, I can't say I was sorry. She had been dangerously stick-happy of late. There was some talk of confiscating it, but nobody was prepared to volunteer.

"She *talked* to you?"

"Not exactly. She complained about the sprouts. Got a bit tetchy when I went near her stick. Said people want to steal it from her. Most of the time she just sat and stared out the window."

"Well," I said, "all I can say is, you got off lightly. Talking of getting off, can you skip work for an hour?"

"Sure. Why?"

"I need your help. There's a mirror I want bringing down from the attic and putting in my laboratory."

"What d'you want a mirror in your lab for?"

"It's not for me. I'm planning to give it to Scarlettine for a wedding present."

"But I thought you didn't – Hey! This is part of your revenge plan, right?"

"Right."

"So how does this mirror fit in? Is it Magic or something?" He sounded quite eager.

"Right again."

"Cool. Hey, I really dig this Magic stuff. Can we get Vanished again sometime?"

"No. Shall we go?"

"OK. So what's so special about this mirror? What does it do? Can you walk through it or what? Hey, that'd be neat."

"Keep your voice down, will you? I want to keep it a secret. Come on. I'll tell you on the way."

"Deal." He looked up at the belfry window and gave a cheery little wave. "'Bye, Grandma!"

I wasn't sure, but I thought I saw the curtain twitch again. I half expected green fire to come whizzing down, or at the very least a bucket of water – but nothing happened.

"I think she likes me," said Alvis cheerfully. "Come on, Buster." And off we set, with Kissy-Woo bouncing happily at our heels.

"There you go," said Alvis, standing back, mopping his brow. "One Magic Mirror."

We were in my laboratory. Between us, we had just carried the Mirror all the way down from the attic –

no mean feat, I can tell you. Actually, Alvis had gallantly done the carrying. I had held doors open and sympathized when he had banged his head on various rafters and low archways. What had made it particularly difficult was the fact that he had to avoid touching the surface. Touching the surface would have awoken Ogggg, who would doubtless have made a fuss. It was a hard enough job as it was without *him* putting in his two penn'orth.

"Thanks," I said. I folded my arms and waited for him to go.

"No problem. Now what?"

"You go. I've got work to do."

"What, no demonstration?"

"No."

"I don't get to meet Ogggg? After all you've told me about him?"

"No. Consider yourself lucky."

"Hey." Alvis was clearly disappointed. "Uncool."

"Look, I just don't want to waste time going over old ground. I've got as far as I can with Scarlettine. Everything's in place. I really need to concentrate on Frostia now."

"Yeah? Great. Like, what are you going to do?"

"Well, first, I'm going to check on Little Gerda. I've been feeling a bit guilty about her actually. I'm hoping to pick her up on my new Crystal Ball."

"Can I help?"

"No. Crystal Gazing is a one-person kind of thing."

"Ah, go on. I helped get the Mirror down."

"Oh, all right. But get Kissy-Woo out of here. She's

messing around with my Magic Cords, look."

"OK. Hey, Buster. Out."

Kissy-Woo looked a bit sad, but trotted out obediently enough. Alvis was working wonders on her. I got the Crystal Ball and sat at my bench. Alvis came and leaned over my shoulder.

"Don't hum," I told him. "It's putting me off. I need to concentrate."

It was true. There is an art to Crystal Gazing. You have to clear your mind of all the stuff that usually clutters it up – what's for dinner, in my case – stare deeply into the Ball and think hard about what it is you want to see.

This new Ball was *good*. There's no doubt that you get what you pay for. Instantly, the mists cleared and I found myself staring down into a miniature, snowy landscape. In the background was Frostia's palace. Even I have to admit that it's impressive. It's all made of ice and set amongst pine trees, with a terrific view of snow-capped mountains. At night, it's illuminated by the Northern Lights. Right now, however, it was daytime. A tiny, red-nosed figure was trudging through the snow, towards the rearing gates. I noticed that the silly kid didn't have a scarf on, despite my advice. Still, she had made it to the North Pole. Credit where it was due.

"Is that Little Gerda?" asked Alvis eagerly.

Instantly, the small figure stopped in her tracks and looked around, startled.

"Yes. Shush. Keep your voice down."

"What – you mean she can hear me?"

"Of course she can hear you. This is the latest model. It's got audio facilities."

"What?"

"Audio facilities. You get sound."

"Yeah? Hey! Great! *Hi there, Gerda! This is Alvis speaking! Do you copy? I repeat, do you copy?*"

"Alvis! Will you *please* stop interfering? You'll only confuse her. Move *back*, will you, I can't see a thing."

"Who's there?" came Gerda's tiny, frightened voice. It sounded a bit fuzzy around the edges, but, considering the distance, the reproduction wasn't at all bad.

"Now see!" I hissed crossly. "You've frightened her. Stand back and leave this to me." I gave him a little shove, cleared my throat and spoke clearly. "Hello, Gerda. Wilma here. We met in the forest, remember? I said I'd help you."

"Wilma? Is it really you? But where are you? I can't see you. I just hear ghostly voices squabbling in the wind."

"I've just located you in my Crystal Ball," I explained. "Sorry I've taken so long. How was the journey?"

"Awful. I was set on by robbers and my muff got pinched and I'm only a *little* girl. Everyone kept giving me false directions. I've been so scared and cold and I've only got half a cheese sandwich left."

"Yes, well, you can tell me the details some other time. I see you're nearly there. We don't want to waste time, do we? Now, listen. Don't – I repeat, *don't* attempt going in by the front gates. You'll get challenged by the guards. Go round the back, to the tradesmen's entrance. The gate's quite low, you can climb over it. Keep to the left. Watch out for the wolves. Go to the back door. There's a spare key under a potted holly bush. When you get inside, take the passage to the left. That'll lead you to the Great Hall. Your friend's in there. He'll need thawing. A warm flannel would be best, but in the absence of that, you could try weeping over him a bit. A hot tear or two should do the trick. When he comes round, make a run for it. And when you get home safely, tell him not to talk to strange women in sleighs in future."

"But what if she's there? Your sister, I mean?"

"She's not. She's out with Mother, shopping for new shoes for a wedding. Frostia's got huge feet. They'll take for ever."

"Good luck, Gerda!" shouted Alvis, over my shoulder.

"Who was that?" asked Gerda.

"Nobody important. A friend. Off you go, before you catch cold." And I passed my hand over the Ball, cutting the connection.

"Wilma," said Alvis, "you're all heart."

"I know," I said rather smugly. Well, I had a right to be pleased with myself. For once, things were going my way. If all went according to plan, when Frostia got home she would find herself short of one kidnapped boy. Plus, the business with the Mirror was going well. Now all I had to do was sit back and let things take their course.

I didn't have long to wait.

*

"Something simply ghastly has happened!" announced Mother the following morning, at the breakfast table.

There were only three of us there. Four, if you include Peevish. Grandma was still refusing to come out of the belfry and Uncle Bacchus was in his own castle for once. I think he was getting tired of all the wedding talk.

"I've just had a call from poor Frostia. The boy's escaped!"

"Who?" asked Daddy.

"The boy! The kidnapped boy! He's escaped!"

"Good," said Daddy, and carried on reading the newspaper.

"Deary me," I said, looking up from my porridge. "Surely not? Tut, tut. However did that happen?"

"That's just it! She doesn't know! The poor girl arrived home after our shopping trip – which wasn't very successful, I might add – only to find two sets of small footprints in the snow, the back door wide open and the boy gone! Can you believe it?"

"Perhaps he was carried off by a polar bear," I suggested innocently.

"Don't be silly, Wilma. Whoever did it was human. And what's more, he had inside information. He knew that the back door's never guarded. He avoided the wolves. He knew where to find the spare key too. He must have just strolled in, bold as brass. Unbelievable."

"Or she," I put in.

"What?"

"I'm just saying it could have been a she."

"Don't be ridiculous. A girl would have more sense than to tangle with Frostia. It was obviously a boy."

"Or a Dwarf," put in Peevish. Mother stared at him. "Well, ma'am, you said the footsteps were small."

"Thank you for that observation, Peevish. Anyway, girl, Dwarf, bear, trained monkey, whoever it was, the boy is gone. Frostia is *devastated*. She's shrugging it off and pretending she doesn't care, of course, but I know my own daughter."

"Anything else taken?" inquired Daddy.

"I don't think so. She didn't say."

"That's all right then."

"Oh, George. Have a heart. You know how much that boy meant to her."

"I'm afraid I can't agree with you there, dearest. All he did was sit around spelling out words with bits of ice."

"Yes, but they were quite *long* words. Last week, she tells me, he came up with *marmalade*. Anyway, it's the principle of the thing. It *looks* bad. Just think what it will do to Frostia's reputation if it gets out. And that's not all. The poor darling set off in pursuit and overturned the sleigh in a snow drift! It's a write-off, apparently. That's all she needs, on top of all her problems with the polar ice caps and not managing to find any shoes to fit." She gave a little sigh. "She *does* have such big feet. Where are you going, Wilma?"

"Out. To my room. Nowhere." Actually, I was desperate to find Alvis and break the news to him that the rescue attempt had succeeded.

"Sit down then. I need to talk to you about the wedding."

Reluctantly, I sat down. The last thing I wanted was to talk about the wedding. That's all anyone ever seemed to do lately. There was wedding talk at every mealtime. The whole grotesque affair was being planned down to the last detail. The wedding was to have a red theme. Scarlettine was wearing red apparently, and insisting that Geraldo did too. When the happy couple were pronounced man and wife, seven specially imported scarlet macaws were to be released and seven red-dyed swans were to swim past. The wedding cake was to be three metres high, the bride's train was to be thirty metres long and carried by seven small pageboys in red velvet, blah blah blah . . .

"What about the wedding?" I said warily.

"We need to talk about what you're going to wear."

"What's wrong with my brown dress?"

"Everything. This afternoon, after I've had my sleep, I'm taking you shopping. It's time you had a new outfit. I've seen a nice pink net frock that would . . ."

"Pink *net*?" I howled, horrified. "I'm not wearing pink net. I'd look ridiculous in pink net, wouldn't I, Daddy?"

"I'm just off to see to the tomatoes," said Daddy, folding his newspaper and hurrying out. "I'll leave you girls to sort it out."

Behind him, Mother and I drew up to do battle.

"Pink net," said Mother. "This is your sister's wedding and you will look nice for it."

"Not in pink net, I won't," I declared stoutly.

"I've made up my mind, Wilma. You will wear pink net."

"No," I said. "Never. Not in a million trillion zillion *squillion* years."

# 13. THE WEDDING

"New dress," observed Alvis. "Pink net. Cool."

"Shut up, will you?" I said.

It was the morning of the wedding. We were walking around the side of the Ancestral Halls, having just collected the Mirror from the dungeons. I was striding along in front – in pink net! – and Alvis was trundling the Mirror behind me on his wheelbarrow to where everyone was waiting for Muckbucket to bring the Day Coach round to take us on our merry way.

I was in two minds about today. I wasn't looking forward to the wedding (apart from the cake), but on the other hand I couldn't wait to deliver my wedding gift, which I had thoughtfully gift-wrapped in old newspaper.

Everyone turned to look at us as we approached. They were all decked out in their wedding finery. Mother was wearing a sky-blue gown with a matching hat. For once, her Aura was missing. As a result, the sun was shining and the birds were chirping. It seemed odd to see her off duty.

Daddy and Uncle Bacchus each gave me a little wave. Daddy was looking uncomfortably smart in a new suit. Uncle Bacchus had a new toga and had twined carnations around his vine-leaf coronet. Grandma looked the same as usual, with the addition of a sprout in her buttonhole. It was the first time she had emerged in weeks. We were all rather hoping her temper might have improved after all that self-imposed solitude, but one look at her face told me that this was not to be. Wedding or not, Grandma was still sulking.

"Ah! There you are, Wilma!" cried Mother, relieved. "Oh, *darling*. You could have washed your hair."

"I did," I said. Well, I had. A couple of weeks ago.

"Hmm. Must you wear those old boots? They don't exactly go with your lovely new dress." She would have said more, but just then, her eye was caught by something just past my shoulder. "What in the world is *that*?"

"It's my gift to Scarlettine and Geraldo," I said, all innocence. "It's an antique mirror. It cost a fortune. I hope they like it."

"Oh. Well, that's very sweet, darling, but I don't think there's room for it in the coach. Not now we have to make a detour to pick up Frostia. Her new sleigh hasn't been delivered yet, so she's without transport. By the way, Wilma, don't mention anything about her losing the boy, will you? She's still very touchy about it."

"Oh no," I lied, making a mental note to bring it up at the first opportunity. "As if I would."

"Anyway, that means there will be five of us in the coach, and with that mirror, I just don't think . . ."

"What's the problem?" said Daddy, strolling up. "Well, look at you, pet. All done up in pink net." I thought he would go on to say that I was as pretty as a picture, but he didn't. Well, I wasn't. Quite frankly, I looked a fright.

"I was just telling Wilma that I don't think we can all fit into the coach."

"Can't she follow on behind in the second coach with Peevish and Mrs Pudding?"

"Oh, I don't think so, George. They're bringing all the wedding presents. And The Cake."

"Ah yes," said Daddy. "Of course. I had forgotten The Cake."

The Cake had been made by Mrs Pudding, who considered it her masterpiece. It was three metres high and covered with red icing. Two smirking figurines stood on the top, beneath a miniature sugar arch. It was clear that it would need at least two seats of its own.

"I'll bring Miss Wilma if you like, sir," offered Alvis, who had been hovering around in the background. "I'll harness up the pony and cart, shall I?"

"There's a good lad," said Grandma unexpectedly.

We were all startled. It was the first time she'd had a good word for anybody in – well, years!

Mother seemed to notice Alvis for the first time.

"Who's this?" she said sharply.

"This is young Alvis, who helps in the garden," explained Daddy. "He's very reliable. Thank you, Alvis. That would be splendid."

"Oh, but, George. We can't have Wilma turning up in a *cart*. This is a *wedding* . . ."

She was interrupted by the arrival of the Day Coach. In an attempt to be festive, Muckbucket had gone mad with scarlet ribbons. Even the horses were done up with big red bows like chocolate boxes. Uncle Bacchus ran over to hold the door open.

"Come on then, my lot!" he roared genially. "Step on it!"

"Oh dear!" fretted Mother. "A *cart*, George. I really don't think . . ."

"Go on," I said. "I'll be fine. We'll park it behind some trees. Nobody will see."

"But you don't even know the way."

"I'll get a map. Alvis can drive, and I'll navigate. Go *on*, Mother. I'll be there."

"Well, all right. But whatever happens, don't be late."

"I won't," I promised.

Famous last words.

I *was* late, of course. Everything conspired against us. Alvis insisted on changing into his spangled jacket and blue shoes. I didn't stop him. After all, I looked ridiculous. Why shouldn't he? It took ages to find a map, and ages more to get the pony harnessed up.

Finally we set off, only to realize that we had left the Mirror behind. Back we went, loaded it on and set out once again. Alvis drove like a maniac, but we still got there late, mainly because of my poor attempts at map-reading. Well, how was I to know that the little blue wiggly things are rivers?

King Geraldo's palace was exactly as I had expected: a huge, flashy wedding cake of a place with far too many turrets and towers than were good for it. There were pillars and friezes and mouldings and curly bits. Somebody had slapped on gold leaf as though there was no tomorrow. The place looked ready to collapse under a surfeit of ornamentation. *Look at me!* it seemed to scream. *My owner's got a lot of money, oh yes!* The grounds were the same. Statues, fountains, gazebos, a thumping great swimming pool – you name it, Geraldo had it.

We came crashing up the mile-long drive, soaking wet, just as the bells rang out and the happy couple emerged on the steps. Scarlettine, wearing enough red chiffon to blind a herd of bulls, was waving triumphantly to the hundreds of cheering guests under a rain of red confetti. Everyone was there. The place was stiff with all manner of kings, queens, lords, ladies and minor deities. All Mother's friends were there, plus all Scarlettine's horrible old school chums and a great many people I didn't know, who I presume were friends of the groom.

Geraldo stood at Scarlettine's side, looking very hot and bothered in a tight red velvet doublet, puffy red shorts and matching hose. His face was scarlet too.

Swap his crown for a pair of horns and give him a tail and he could have been a visiting demon from you know where. Behind them, on the steps, a dozen small, red-garbed pageboys were hanging on to Scarlettine's train. One had a nose bleed and was using the train to mop it up.

My family were very much in evidence, of course. Daddy was gently patting Mother, who was dabbing at her eyes with a hanky. Uncle Bacchus was cheering and waving a flag. Frostia was yawning as if she was bored stiff by the proceedings and Grandma was leaning on her stick and glaring daggers at everybody. Peevish and Mrs Pudding were there too. Peevish had a new suit, I noticed, and Mrs Pudding was wearing her best Bingo hat.

Nobody noticed our arrival. There was far too much cheering and general celebration going on. We parked discreetly behind a clump of trees. I left Alvis to unload the Mirror and tried to blend quietly into the crowd. Instantly, I was pounced upon by Soggy, Puffer and Rumbleguts.

"Wilma!" shrieked Soggy. "*There* you are! Where have you *been*? Your mother is most displeased with you."

"Quite right too," sniffed Puffer. "Missing your own sister's wedding. Whatever next?"

"Such a lovely service too," added Rumbleguts.

The three of them stared at me accusingly.

"Got a bit lost," I mumbled. "By the way, did you know Frostia's kidnapped boy has been rescued? By a *little girl*. Don't spread it around, she's terribly embarrassed. Excuse me. I've just seen someone I know." And I pushed my way through the crowd to where Snow White was standing. She was leaning against a tree, all on her own, watching Scarlettine and Geraldo pose on the steps while the court artists scribbled flattering lightning sketches. Her lower lip was trembling and her eyes were red.

"Hello, Snow White. Remember me? Ghastly, isn't it?" I said sociably. From the corner of my eye I noticed Soggy, Puffer and Rumbleguts excitedly rushing about, whispering in people's ears. Good.

"Mmm. I cried all night. Oh, Wilma, what am I going to *do*? Things will be even worse now they're married. I just know it. Father will have no time for me at all now *she's* got her hooks in him."

She nodded towards Scarlettine, who had just thrown her bouquet of red roses to the waiting crowd. It hit little Lord Loser in the eye, which caused a bit of a laugh. Everyone then started to make their way to the ornamental lake so that the court artists could get another sketch opportunity. Snow White and I drifted behind in their wake.

"Come on," I said. "Cheer up. Everything's going to be fine."

"It is?" She gazed at me hopefully.

"You bet. I've got a surprise wedding present for Scarlettine. In fact, here it comes now."

"Hey," said Alvis, advancing towards us with the Mirror clasped in his arms. The newspaper was beginning to become a bit unravelled, I noticed. It was more like something off a rubbish tip than a desirable wedding present. "Where d'you want this?"

"What is it?" asked Snow White with curiosity.

"It's Alvis. The boy with the strange haircut I told you about before."

"No, I mean, what's the present?"

I was just about to tell her when there came a diversion. The time had come for the seven specially imported macaws to do their fly past, but it wasn't happening quite the way it was supposed to. Annoyed at being cooped up, they came squawking out of their cage in battle formation, attacking several of the wedding guests and releasing an unpleasant shower of guano on all and sundry before zooming off over the tree tops, never to be seen again.

The swans weren't much better. They obviously hadn't enjoyed being dyed red. They categorically refused to swim, preferring to launch themselves at their handler and peck him quite badly. Cross swans are worth seeing, I can tell you. Especially when they're hanging on to someone else's trousers. Alvis and I nearly died laughing. Even Snow White giggled a bit, particularly when she saw Scarlettine's furious face.

After all these amusing lakeside capers, a flunkey's announcement that the wedding feast was about to be served in the Banqueting Hall came as quite an anti-climax.

Even the food had a red theme, can you believe? It was a buffet with lobster, beetroot, strawberries and lots of red apples, which are Scarlettine's favourite. Mrs Pudding's towering red cake had pride of place in the middle. Alvis and I placed the Mirror on the sideboard, which was groaning with beautifully wrapped offerings. It stood out a bit.

"You were about to tell me what it is," Snow White reminded me as we stood back, panting a bit.

"A Magic Mirror," I said. "The instrument of Scarlettine's doom. There's a Trapped Spirit inside, and I've bribed him to be on our side. Now, here's what you have to do . . ."

And I told her. She listened carefully, just nodding occasionally until I got to the end.

"That's it," I finished. "Any questions?"

"Just one. Does it have to be bears? I'm not sure I fancy living with bears."

"No, no. I just said bears as an example. It's up to you who you hide out with."

"But supposing I don't get any offers?"

"Snow White," I said, rather snappishly, I'm afraid, "as you well know, you *are* rather pretty. All you have to do is sit beneath a tree and sob helplessly, and before you know it, the place will be awash with do-gooders offering you a roof over your head in return for a song, a dance and a maybe a little light housework. You'll be just fine. Besides, I'll be keeping an eye on you with my Crystal Ball. Are you up for it or not?"

Snow White glanced across the room at Scarlettine, who was merrily laughing and feeding King Geraldo from a bowl of strawberries.

"Yes," she said. "I am. I'll do anything to get rid of *her*."

"Good. We'd better split up now. We don't want

people to notice us talking too much. Come on, Alvis. Let's get some cake."

We made our way to the buffet. Frostia was standing by a pillar, looking even more fed up than usual.

"You're in trouble," she sneered as I came up. "Mother is furious you were so late. What were you doing talking to that Snow White girl?"

"None of your business," I retorted, adding loudly, "I hear the kidnapped boy's escaped. What a shame."

"Keep your voice down, will you? I don't want the whole world to know."

"Oh, but I'm only being sympathetic. You must feel really silly. Someone in your position. Being foiled by a *little girl*."

"How do you know that? Did you have something to do with it?"

"Me? Perish the thought."

"Then how do you know it was a girl?"

"Oh, just rumours. I expect you miss the boy a lot?"

"Not particularly. Actually, I couldn't care less. With winter coming on, I'll be much too busy to bother about him."

Icy mists were gathering about her. It was like standing next to an open freezer. She was furious about it. Good.

As I remarked to Alvis on the way home, things were beginning to work out quite well.

# 14. THE PLOT THICKENS

I got into serious trouble, of course. Mother was absolutely furious with me. I was confined to my room for two days as a punishment. I didn't care. I'd had a busy time recently. Revenge is tiring. I quite enjoyed lying around in bed, scoffing biscuits and having my meals delivered on a tray. Denzil came to join me, and together we would sit by the window, watching the clouds go by and occasionally waving to Alvis as he went about his duties in the grounds.

On the third day, I put on my old brown dress and went down to breakfast. Mother and Daddy were seated at the table. Rather to my surprise, so was Scarlettine. For someone newly married, she didn't look very happy.

"Good morning, Wilma," said Mother. "We have a surprise visitor for breakfast. Your sister! Isn't that *lovely*?"

"What's she doing here?" I inquired ungraciously. "I thought she was on her honeymoon."

"I cut it short, if you must know," said Scarlettine. "I was getting bored. That's *another* thing, Mother. Geraldo spent the entire time sending postcards with stupid rabbits on to Snow White. And he won't hear of us confining her to a tower. He actually *argued* with me about it, can you believe?"

"Oh dear," I said. "The course of true love not running as smoothly as you'd like?"

"Shut up, Wilma. I'm talking to Mother. I don't see why I should even *speak* to you after the beastly wedding present you gave me."

"Didn't you like it?" I inquired innocently.

"Of course I didn't! Ugly, cheap old thing. Besides, it doesn't even work properly. That Spirit has a real personality problem."

"Work properly?" inquired Mother, brow wrinkling. "Spirit? What are we talking about here?"

"Wilma knows. I'm talking about the stupid old Magic Mirror she gave me."

"Magic?" Mother stared at me hard. "I didn't know it was Magic."

"Oh," I said vaguely. "Didn't I mention it?"

"It's rubbish anyway," continued Scarlettine, with a scowl. "It's got a stupid old Spirit trapped in it who only answers the one stupid question. And it can't even get *that* right."

"Oh-ho," I said knowingly. "Answer not to your liking then?"

"What's the question?" asked Mother.

"Who Is the Fairest One of All?" I said cheerfully, adding, "From the look on Scarlettine's face, I gather it's not her."

"It is!" snapped Scarlettine, going bright red. "I *am* the fairest! Tell her, Mother!"

"Of course you are, darling," soothed Mother. "No one can hold a candle to you. Take no notice of Wilma's nasty Mirror. What does a silly old Spirit know?"

"Exactly! The stupid thing got it right to begin with, then it . . . it . . ." Scarlettine was so angry she couldn't get the words out.

"What?" urged Mother. "It what? Tell us, darling. You'll feel better."

"*It said Snow White!*" screamed Scarlettine. Red fire suddenly spurted from her fingertips and the milk jug exploded. She was seriously put out, you could tell.

"There, there, darling," soothed Mother, patting her arm. "Try not to use Magic at the table, you know Daddy doesn't like it. Cheer up. I'm sure it didn't *mean* it."

"I think it did, you know," I popped in. "Trapped Spirits don't tell lies. It goes against the Trapped Spirit code."

"Thank you for that, Wilma," said Mother coldly. "I shall speak to you later."

"Anyway," continued Scarlettine, shooting me a look with arrows in, "anyway, I've had enough of Snow White. I'm taking matters into my own hands. I'm getting rid of her."

"Scarlettine!" interrupted Daddy. "I'm surprised at you! That really is taking things too far!"

"The farther the better, as far as I'm concerned. There's no point in going on about it, Daddy. I've made up my mind. I'm going to have a word with Geraldo's chief huntsman. I shall command him to get his sharpest knife and take her into the forest and . . ."

"No!" shouted Daddy. He was as cross as I've ever seen him. "I forbid it. You are not to touch one hair of that poor young lass's head!"

"Now, now, George. Sit down, dearest, you'll get indigestion." Mother gave Scarlettine a warning look and put her finger to her lips. "Scarlettine, I don't think now is the time or place, do you? You know Daddy doesn't like to hear the details. Let's all talk about something else, shall we? I'll tell you what I've been thinking. It's Frostia's birthday next week. She's been rather down lately. On top of the missing boy business, her palace has got shocking subsidence. It's this global warming we keep hearing about. Cracks appearing everywhere. She can't move without chunks of ice falling on her head. I thought it would be nice to give her a surprise party. What do you think?"

"I think she should get in some proper builders and get it sorted out," said Daddy.

"Oh, George. That's not Frostia's way, you know that. She'll never admit she's beaten. She's holding it all together by Magic, but it's taking its toll. She's getting shocking migraines and having to pay the staff danger money. A party is just what she needs to cheer her up. What do you think?"

There was a little silence while we all thought

about this. Frostia hates being cheerful. There was nothing she would dislike more than having us turn up all jolly on her doorstep, waving balloons and threatening her with a surprise party. Particularly with a melting palace on her hands. But I had the glimmerings of an idea. This might be the very opportunity I needed to put the finishing touches to my glorious revenge.

"Good idea," I said heartily. "We could take along a hamper, couldn't we? And some jolly squeakers, don't you think?"

"Well, yes, Wilma, we could. A hamper would be a lovely thought. I'm not so sure about the squeakers though. The palace is very unstable. The least noise could bring it tumbling down around our ears. I thought we could all go in the Night Coach. It'll kill two birds with one stone."

And so the conversation turned away from Scarlettine's wicked plans. It didn't matter. I knew enough to warn Snow White. As soon as I could, I made my excuses and went down to my lab and got out my Crystal Ball.

"Snow White," I said urgently, as soon as she swam into view. "It's me." I noted that even though she was in the process of cleaning out the rabbit hutch, she looked as neat and clean as ever.

"Fluffy!" she gasped, staring at the rabbit. "I didn't know you could talk!"

Honestly. I wonder about her sometimes.

"It's not Fluffy," I said tiredly. "It's Wilma."

"Wilma? But where are you?"

"I'm looking at you in my Crystal Ball. Is anyone around? Can we talk?"

"Well, yes. I'm all alone. As usual." Tears welled up in her eyes.

"Don't waste time crying, there's a good girl. Now, listen carefully. Everything's going according to plan. The Mirror's done its job and Scarlettine's wild with jealousy and determined to get rid of you. But there's a complication. She's going to get the chief huntsman to do her dirty work."

"What? Faithful old Roger? But he's *sweet*. Roger would never hurt me. We're great friends."

"Glad to hear it. But Scarlettine doesn't know that. The best thing is for you both to go along with it, right? Faithful old Roger takes you into the forest and leaves you there. Then he goes back and tells Scarlettine that he's done the dastardly deed. Meanwhile, you hole up in the forest and wait until you hear from me. Got that?"

"All right," she said, with a little sigh. "But it's rotten."

"I know," I said. "But it's all for the good of the cause."

"But what if it's raining?"

"Take an umbrella." And I swiftly cut the connection, before she could change her mind.

The following week flew by. Well, I had a lot to do. To begin with, I had to organize Frostia's birthday present. Alvis came in handy there. There was something very specific I wanted and he gave me a lot of useful advice.

We spent ages poring through catalogues and finally came up with the very thing. We had quite a bit of catching up to do because I hadn't seen much of him since the wedding. I told him all about Scarlettine's plan and he was duly horrified. He didn't like the idea of the poor girl hiding out in the forest at all. If he hadn't been so tied up with his gardening duties and the daily sprout delivery to the belfry, I think he would have set off to look for her there and then.

"Why does Grandma like you so much?" I inquired with curiosity. We were sitting in his bare room at the time. Alvis was strumming his guitar and I was admiring my gift for Frostia, which had arrived that morning. It was perfect. Everything I had hoped for. I couldn't wait to give it to her.

"I dunno," he said, with a little shrug.

"You took your guitar up there the other day, didn't you? I saw you."

"Yeah, well, she gets bored with nothing to do all day. Ma says there's nothing worse than idle hands. Idle hands make for an idle brain, she reckons."

"Does she?" I asked. "Well, I dare say she's right. I'd like to meet your ma one day, Alvis."

"Mmmm." He put down his guitar, stretched and stood up. "Well, I'd best be off. Lunchtime's over. Gotta make with the shears in the lower orchard. See you round, Wilma. Come on, Buster." And with that, he was gone.

I wondered briefly whether to go down to my lab and try once again to raise Snow White on my Crystal Ball, but then decided against it. I'd tried several times recently, with no success. All I got was swirling mists. After the fourth attempt, I looked at the instructions and found a warning written in small print. It said:

*Repeated use of audio facility will drain the power. It is recommended that you allow your Ball to rest for a minimum of three weeks between contacts.*

So much for the cutting edge of Magicology. Oh well. No doubt she was coping all right. People with eyelashes that long always do. Besides, it wouldn't do to rush things. Timing was everything. Geraldo would doubtless be organizing search parties and tearing his hair out by now. I would let him stew in his own juice for a bit.

Anyway, I had plenty to do. Wrap Frostia's present, for a start. I picked it up from the bed and, humming cheerfully, went off to find some newspaper.

# 15. FROSTIA'S BIRTHDAY

The last time I had seen Frostia's palace was in my Crystal Ball, when I was talking to Gerda. It was looking rather splendid then. Not so now. When we alighted stiffly from the Night Coach, we weren't prepared for the sight that met our eyes. Instead of crisp, white snow, the moonlight fell on a sea of grey slush. The palace had a definite tilt to the left. Huge cracks had appeared in its walls. There were several gaping black holes in the roof.

"Good grief," said Daddy. "Take a bit of sorting out, that will."

Shivering, and laden down with hamper, presents and balloons, we waded through the slush to the steep flight of steps leading up to the main doors, which were formed of two enormous, glistening slabs of sheet ice.

It had been a horrible journey. Circling the globe had been a nightmare. Snow, hail, sleet, freezing fog – you name it, we had it. There weren't enough rugs to go round, because Grandma pinched them all. Daddy and Uncle Bacchus had both wanted to smoke cigars, but Mother had forbidden them because of the balloons, so they were both as fidgety as anything. I felt queasy, as I always do when flying. I hate riding in the Night Coach. I don't know how Mother can bear to do it every night. The only good thing was the fact that we didn't have Scarlettine with us. She and Geraldo were making their own way, apparently.

Climbing the steps wasn't fun. They were all melting. Getting Grandma up them was a misery. Every time we got her up two, she slithered back three. Finally, Mother lost patience and used a quick transportation spell to transport us all up to the top step. She doesn't normally like using her supernatural powers around Daddy, but we would have been there all night.

Daddy took out a pen and prodded at a supporting pillar. A large chunk of ice came away. He and Uncle Bacchus shook their heads and muttered darkly to each other in that wise, know-all way that men do when faced with a building that is structurally unsound.

"Don't, George!" hissed Mother. "Do you want the place to come down around our ears? Now, don't forget, we've all got to be jolly. Not *too* jolly, Bacchus. Have you got the balloons, Wilma?"

"Right here," I said, holding them up. Sadly, there

was a holly bush in a pot to my right and all but one burst in a series of sharp little explosions. A mini avalanche of snow slid off the portico and dropped down our necks.

"Ooops," I said. "Sorry."

"Oh *dear*!" sighed Mother.

Uncle Bacchus pulled on the bell rope. A distant, echoing crash like colliding stalactites came from somewhere inside. After what seemed like an age, the door opened a crack.

"Surprise!" we all shouted.

"Oh," said Frostia. She was wearing a white dressing gown and her face was shiny with night cream. "It's you." Her voice held about as much warmth as a duck pond in the ice age.

"Happy birthday, darling!" said Mother, kissing her cold cheek. "We thought we'd give you a surprise visit."

"I was on my way to bed. I haven't got anything in."

"Oh, that's all right. We've brought a lovely hamper, see? And some – a jolly balloon. Give Frostia her balloon, Wilma. Oh dear. That one's popped as well, has it? What a pity."

"I don't have any staff. They've all left. There's no one to serve us."

"No matter, pet. We'll serve ourselves," said Daddy soothingly. And we all filed in.

The floor, once as hard as a skating rink, was a sea of cold, sloshy puddles. We had to step between dozens of overflowing buckets which had been placed at regular intervals in a vain attempt to catch the drips which rained down in a steady stream from the high ceilings.

"Just don't make any loud noises," Frostia warned us. "The roof could go at any time."

Gingerly, we paddled into the main hall, where Frostia has her throne. It's carved from ice and engraved with intricate snowflake patterns. At least, that's how it used to be. Right now, it resembled a large, thawing ice cube set on top of a dripping dais. The white carpet that led up to it squelched unpleasantly every time one put one's foot down.

"I'll just set out the goodies then, shall I?" trilled Mother, determinedly bright and gay. She looked around for somewhere to unload the contents of the hamper.

"There isn't anywhere," said Frostia sulkily. "The table's melted."

"Never mind, we'll have a picnic," said Daddy, trying his best to make it sound like a frolicsome thing to do. "Set it out on the floor, Veronica."

"Oh. Well, yes. Right," said Mother doubtfully. She set a plate of cucumber sandwiches on the sloping floor. It went slithering away into a far corner. "Whoops! Ha ha, this is – er – fun. We've brought you a lovely cake, see? Oh dear, everything's sliding. Bacchus, why don't you find a – lump of ice or something for Mama to sit on? George, give Frostia her presents."

Uncle Bacchus took Grandma's arms and guided her across to a melting blob that had once been an exquisitely carved ice settee. Frostia took her seat on her dripping throne and Daddy placed a box of presents in her lap.

"Go on, love," he urged. "Open 'em up then."

Just then, there came an interruption: the sound of a distant crash, like giant doors slamming shut, followed by the clacking of high heels. This was followed by the sound of a bucket being overturned and a high-pitched scream of fury. Then more footsteps.

Scarlettine had arrived. She was on her own, and in the most terrible temper. She flounced into the hall, earrings jangling like warning bells and lips twisted into a snarl.

"Scarlettine!" cried Mother. "What's wrong, darling? Whatever's happened?"

"*Dwarfs!*" shrieked Scarlettine, at the top of her voice. The word bounced and echoed off the streaming walls. A medium-sized chunk of ice detached itself from the ceiling and fell within centimetres of Uncle Bacchus.

There was a little silence.

"I'm sorry, darling," said Mother. "Did you say, *Dwarfs*?"

"Yes! Yes! Dwarfs! *Seven* of them!" spat Scarlettine. And with another wild shriek, she threw herself full-length on the soaking floor and pummelled it with both fists.

"Come on now, Scarlettine," said Daddy. "Don't be silly, you'll catch your death."

"Daddy's right, darling. Get up, there's a dear. You're getting soaked."

There was a little pause. Then Scarlettine rolled over and sullenly clambered to her feet. She lurched over to the settee and threw herself into it, at the other end from Grandma.

"*Dwarfs!*" she hissed again. "I hate them! With their silly little hats and everything! *Oooh!* I could *scream*!"

"You just did," remarked Frostia cuttingly. "We don't need another one. The ceiling won't stand it."

"Shush, Frostia," said Mother. "Something's happened to Scarlettine. Calm down, darling, and tell us all about it."

She did, of course – in great detail. It took absolutely ages, so I'll sum it up quickly. The gist of it was that she had done what she threatened to do and ordered the chief huntsman (faithful old Roger, of course!) to do away with Snow White. She had then consulted with Ogggg again, only to learn that she had been deceived. Snow White had escaped into the forest and set up home with a load of Dwarfs. (You see? I knew she wouldn't have any trouble finding someone to take pity on her. Seven Dwarfs came as a bit of a surprise though. Even to me.)

Determined to do away with the competition once and for all, Scarlettine had then taken matters into her own hands. She had disguised herself as an old pedlar woman and called twice at the Dwarfs' cottage with tempting goods for sale. These included too-tight corsets, of all things, and a poisoned comb. The bad news (or good, depending on your point of view), was that, both times, Snow White had fallen for the trick. (Typical. After all my warnings.) The good news (or bad) was that on each occasion, the Dwarfs had arrived back in time to revive her.

On top of everything else, Geraldo was beginning to get suspicious. He had stopped showering Scarlettine with gifts and kept asking whether she knew anything about his precious daughter's disappearance. Things were getting quite tense between them, it seemed. Good.

Mother was terribly sympathetic. Daddy just kept shaking his head and sighing a lot. It was clear where his sympathies lay. Grandma just sat upright, glaring straight ahead, and Uncle Bacchus kept casting longing glances at the picnic. Me, I just stood there hugging myself and trying not to grin.

"There, there, Scarlettine," murmured Mother. "Don't despair, darling. I'm sure we can come up with another idea between us. A poisoned banana or something. That's sure to do the trick. *Do* stop gnashing your teeth. I was hoping for a lovely party. Frostia hasn't even opened her presents yet."

"Oh," said Frostia distantly. "Somebody noticed."

"Now, now, darling, don't be like that. Why don't you open them now? I'm sure we're all dying to see.Gather round, everyone!"

Grandma and Scarlettine stayed exactly where they were, sitting at opposite ends of the settee like grim bookends. Daddy, Uncle and I all dutifully gathered around to see what Frostia got.

She had some white gloves from Mother, a fur muff from Daddy, a pair of ice skates from Uncle Bacchus and an ice bucket with a gift tag reading *From Grandma.*

"I never got that," said Grandma. "Darned fool bucket. What would I get that for?"

"Ha, ha, ha," said Mother. "Now then, Mama."

"Is that it?" inquired Frostia ungraciously.

"If you're expecting one from me, think again," snarled Scarlettine. "I've got too much on my mind to be bothered with birthday presents."

"Actually, *I've* got you something," I announced sweetly, and held out the parcel I had been secretly nursing under my cloak.

"Oh, Wilma!" cooed Mother. "That was sweet of you. Isn't that sweet of Wilma, Frostia?"

"What is it?" inquired Frostia, poking at it suspiciously with a silver talon.

"Open it and see." I watched, smiling slightly as she removed the paper to reveal a black box.

Now, as you know, I had gone to a lot of trouble with my present. She reached inside and took it out. It was a trumpet. All new and shiny, with complicated valves and all manner of twiddly bits.

"I thought you might like to take up a musical instrument," I announced into the uncertain silence. "I thought you'd need another hobby. Now the boy's gone."

"Well, bless my soul!" That was Uncle Bacchus. "A trumpet, eh? It's a while since I had a blow on one of these. Used to have trumpet lessons when I was a kid, remember, sis? Give it here, girl, let's see if I can still raise a note." And before anyone could stop him, he had plucked the trumpet from Frostia's hand and was raising it to his mouth.

"Noooooo . . ." wailed Frostia. But she was too late. He pursed up his lips and blew.

A single, cracked, blaring note resounded around the hall. Everyone winced and clapped their hands to their ears as it bounced off the walls. Echo after echo resounded, setting the teeth vibrating unpleasantly in the head.

"You see? You never forget. Bit like riding a bicycle," began Uncle Bacchus, sounding pleased with himself, and took another breath. But before he could play an encore, we became aware of another noise. A sort of cracking, grating sound, accompanied by a distant rumbling.

The buckets containing the icy water began to vibrate. Before our eyes, a great crack appeared in one of the walls. Frostia gave a thin, high scream and leapt to her feet.

"It's falling!" she shrieked. "Watch out! *The roof's caving in!*"

And with that, a gigantic chunk of ice, the size of a grand piano, came hurling down into our midst, closely followed by another, and another. The entire hall was cracking up around us. Great slabs of ice were crashing down everywhere, blocking our way to the door. Luckily, Mother had the presence of mind to utter a quick removing spell. Before we knew it, we were all standing in a little group outside and at a safe distance from the palace, watching it slowly fall apart before our very eyes.

"Oops," muttered Uncle Bacchus, as the tallest tower buckled in the middle and came crashing to the ground in a shower of ice splinters. "Sorry, niece. Shouldn't have blown the trumpet. All my fault."

"No, it isn't," said Frostia, between gritted teeth. "It's Wilma's. She bought the beastly thing. I'm holding her responsible."

"I didn't blow it though," I pointed out truthfully. Well, I hadn't. Although, of course, it must be confessed that I knew in my mind that it would be only a matter of time before somebody would pick it up and give it a blow. A brand-new trumpet is simply irresistible.

"Frostia's quite right, Wilma," agreed Mother coldly. "Of all the unsuitable presents! Whatever made you think of doing such a thing to your own sister? It's very, *very* wicked of you."

"I know," I said. It was freezing standing there in the snow, but inside, I had a warm, warm glow.

# 16. THE REUNION

Mother knows how to hit where it hurts. She did the worse thing she could have done. She confiscated all my Magic stuff. That included the Crystal Ball, so I couldn't keep tabs on Snow White. Mind you, there was no shortage of information. For the next few days, the talk at the dinner table was of nothing else other than Scarlettine's desperate attempts to get rid of the poor girl.

Disguised as an old pedlar woman, she had taken herself along to the Dwarfs' cottage, armed with a poisoned apple (not banana, as Mother had suggested). Snow White had been deceived yet *again*. Honestly, you could run rings around that girl. Pretty she might be. Smart she isn't. I confess I was rather concerned when I heard this. But I cheered up when, a few days later, Mother came up with another interesting piece of news.

It seems that the Dwarfs had stuck Snow White into a glass coffin, of all weird things. A strange idea, but Dwarfs are a law unto themselves, as anyone will tell you. Then, blow me down if some *prince* didn't come riding by. Talk about luck. Some things you just can't anticipate. He was rather taken with Snow White apparently, and wanted to take her home with him. When the coffin was lifted, the piece of poisoned apple fell from her mouth and she sat up, right as rain. Then the prince carried her off into the sunset on his charger and now there was talk of them getting married.

"Good," said Daddy, when he heard this.

"*George!* How *could* you!" cried Mother. "Poor Scarlettine. This horrid prince has only written a *stinking* letter to Geraldo accusing Scarlettine of all kinds of nasty things. The poor girl's beside herself."

"Well, let's hope it teaches her a lesson," said Daddy. "I always said she'd go too far one day, and now she has."

"But, *George* . . ."

I listened to it all and wisely refrained from commenting. I wasn't exactly in the running for Most Popular Daughter of the Month. It was time to keep a low profile. Of course, at every fresh snippet of news, I'd go rushing off to tell Alvis. There's no fun in somebody else's downfall unless you can tell a friend about it and snigger at the best bits.

Then, a few days later, something rather shocking happened. Alvis went missing.

"Have you seen young Alvis, Miss Wilma?" inquired Mrs Pudding, sticking her head out of the kitchen door. "It's time for him to take the Queen Mother's sprouts up."

"No," I said. "He's probably out in the grounds somewhere. I'll go and see."

He wasn't in the grounds. I checked the rose garden, the lake, the stables, the kitchen garden – everywhere. I poked my nose into the potting shed, where Daddy had his feet up and was reading the latest issue of *Tomato World*.

"Have you seen Alvis, Daddy?" I inquired.

"Funnily enough, I haven't. It's not like him to be late. Perhaps he's overslept."

"Maybe. I'll go and give him a knock."

But he wasn't in his room either. Getting no response to my thunderous pounding, I opened the door. The room was bare. No guitar. No jar of hair grease. Just his gardening clothes, hanging neatly on a wire hanger. Oh, and a note on the bed. Slowly, I picked it up and unfolded it. This is what it said:

*Wilma. We're moving on, Ma and me. I'm no good at goodbyes. Hope you understand. Look after Buster for me and say sorry to your dad. Stay cool. Alvis.*

That was it. I studied it for a long time. Then I put it in my pocket and went back to the kitchen.

"Found him, have you?" asked Mrs Pudding.

"No," I said.

"Oh, bother the boy. Where is he? Your grandma's getting herself into a right old lather. Bangin' on the windows, she is. An' it's Mr Peevish's day off. I suppose

I'll 'ave to take 'er sprouts up meself."

"Give them to me," I said. "I'll go. I've nothing better to do."

"Are you all right?" said Mrs Pudding.

"Fine," I lied.

"It's just that you seem a bit low."

"I said I'm fine."

And I took the steaming bowl and left the kitchen without another word.

Grandma was sitting in her rocking chair, as always. She looked up sharply as I entered her room. Pat, Matt and Hatty immediately left the curtain rail and fluttered up to the rafters, where they attached themselves to a beam and hung.

"Where's the boy?" snapped Grandma. "I didn't ask for you. Where's young Alvis?"

I pulled a small table across to her chair and set the sprouts down.

"Gone," I said.

"Gone? Gone where? What d'you mean gone?"

I took the note from my pocket and handed it to her. She stared down at it, jaws working.

"Well I'm jiggered," she said finally, letting it fall on her lap. "Just like that, eh?"

"Just like that," I said. A little silence fell.

"What's he thinkin' of, takin' off like that? I talks to him. Who am I gonna talk to now?"

"I'm here. You can talk to me."

"What would I wanna do that for? You don't make me chuckle. The boy makes me chuckle. We had lots o' chuckles, him an' me. He had time for an old woman. Not like some."

I gave a little sigh. This was getting nowhere.

"Right," I said. "I might as well go then." And I moved to the door.

I was just about to leave, when Grandma said, "How are your revenge plans comin' along?"

"What?" I said, stopping short.

"You heard. Now you're here, you might as well catch me up on the news. I wants to know how your revenge plans is goin'. On them sisters of yours."

"What do you know about it?"

"More'n you think." Grandma gave a sly little titter. "I knows about vanishin' the dog. An' rescuin' the boy. The trumpet was a good one. I enjoyed that. Subtle. I knew Bacchus'd fall for that one. Never could resist a bit o' noise, Bacchus. Givin' that old Mirror to Scarlettine was good too. I gotta hand it to you."

"Did Alvis tell you all this?"

"'Course. But he ain't here no more, so *you* tell me. I wants to know about Scarlettine. She's had it comin' to her a long time, that young madam. Too smug by half. An' Frostia's too snooty. Gang up on you, don't they? I don't blame you for wantin' to get yer own back. I trust things 'ave come to a satisfactory conclusion?"

Wonders would never cease! It was becoming very clear that Grandma was a lot more on the ball than we'd been giving her credit for.

"Well," I said, "if you *really* want to know . . ."

And I told her the recent developments. I related

Scarlettine's final visit to the Dwarfs' cottage with the poisoned apple, the business with the coffin and the prince and the fact that there was another wedding in the offing.

"Well," said Grandma, somewhat wistfully, "a happy endin' for Snow White then. All right for some. I suppose Scarlettine's in the doghouse with that dodgy little red chap she married?"

"You mean King Geraldo. Yep. He's chucked her out," I said, with a grin. "Mother told us over breakfast this morning. She's back in her own castle, sulking. She's pretending she doesn't care, but I bet she does. I've got a feeling there won't be so many princes lining up to claim her hand in marriage from now on. The word gets round."

"And Frostia? What's the news there?"

"She's renting an igloo while her palace is being rebuilt," I reported, with grim satisfaction. "Mother says she's not enjoying it much."

"Good. Serve her right for bein' so stuck up." Grandma gave a little chuckle. "You been a busy girl, Wilma. I couldn't have done better meself. Reckon we'll make a Wicked Queen of you yet."

"Thanks, Grandma," I said, surprised. She had never paid me a compliment before. "Mother says I'll have to do something about my hair first."

"Oh, the hair don't matter. It's how you feel inside. How *do* you feel inside? Now you've got your revenge?"

"Great."

"Not even a little touch of guilt?"

"No fear. As far as I'm concerned, they deserve everything they got."

"True. Not everybody does, mind." She gave a little sigh and her eyes turned to the picture hanging backwards against the wall. "Sometimes, people don't deserve what they gets. You've gotta be sure they do before you doles out justice. You gotta live with it afterwards."

A little silence fell. I decided to grab the bull by the horns. After all, we'd been getting on just fine. I don't think I had ever had a proper conversation with Grandma before. She seemed to know all my secrets. It was time I knew hers.

"You're talking about Aunt Maud, aren't you?" I said.

I half expected her to pick up her stick and try to zap me again. But she didn't. Much to my surprise, a single tear brimmed over and trickled down her wrinkled cheek.

"I shouldn't have pushed her," she said. "She weren't cut out for the job. She'd never have made a Queen. I should have accepted her for what she was. She were my daughter an' I drove 'er away. I shouldn't have done it, Wilma. I realized that when I'd calmed down. I tried to find her, you know. I never told no one, but I did. I used all me Magical Arts. But no one could find Maudie when she didn't want to be found."

"There, there," I muttered. "Don't upset yourself." I was used to Grandma being angry. I had never seen her sad before and I didn't like it. She fumbled in her pocket and brought out a hanky.

"I've never said that before," she muttered, blowing her nose. "Not to no one. Everyone thinks I'm just a crazy, bad-tempered old woman. But I'd give the world for her to walk into this room now. My little Maudie. Gone with the Sprouts. No one knows how much I miss her."

A silence fell. I stood around awkwardly, not knowing what to do.

"What was she like?" I said, at length.

"Free as a bird. Ran around collectin' wild flowers an' herbs an' stuff. Good with animals. Sang folk songs. Very musical."

"No, I mean, what did she look like?"

"Take a look." Grandma nodded to the painting. I hesitated. "Go on. I won't zap you, if that's what you're thinkin'."

I walked over to the painting, reached up and hooked it off the rail. I turned it round, leaned it carefully against the wall and stood back.

So. This was my Aunt Maud. She was sitting cross-legged on a grassy hillock, wearing a green dress. A poppy was tucked into her long brown hair. Her fingers were poised over the strings of a conker-brown guitar.

"That's her," said Grandma. "That's my Maud. Pretty, weren't she? Pestered me for months for that guitar, she did. The boy had a guitar, you know. Brought it up and played for me sometimes. I couldn't see him clearly – me old eyes ain't what they were – but I loved hearin' 'im. Did you know?"

"Yes," I said. "I did."

"I could never hear it without thinkin' of her. 'Course, I never let on. What d'you think? Remind you of your ma, does she?"

I stared long and hard at the smiling face before me. I could see the Family resemblance, of course. She did look a little like Mother. But there was somebody else she reminded me of much, much more.

"Excuse me, got to go!" I shouted – and raced from the room.

My thoughts were whirling as I clattered down the belfry stairs. I hadn't a clue where to start. I knew they lived in a caravan, Alvis and his ma, but beyond that, I knew nothing. Where was the caravan parked? Would anyone know? Why had I never asked these things?

I decided to make for the potting shed. If anyone knew, Daddy would. I was just about to race off when I heard a little whimper. Kissy-Woo was sitting in the flower bed at the base of the belfry. She had something between her paws.

"What's that you've got there?" I said.

Kissy-Woo looked up, gave another little whine and hopefully wagged her tail.

It was Alvis's straw hat, the one he used for gardening. I picked it up.

"Where's he gone, girl? Where's Alvis?"

At the sound of his name, she broke into an excited yapping. I thrust the hat under her nose.

"Go on, Buster! Find! Find Alvis!"

She yapped again, ran away a few metres, came back, tugged at the hem of my dress, then streaked away across the lawns and down the driveway towards the main gates without a backward glance. Behind and up above me, the belfry window rattled open.

"What *are* you playin' at, Wilma?" shouted Grandma.

But I was already in hot pursuit. I didn't stop to reply.

I'm not used to running. I was gasping for breath by the time I reached the main gates. I sagged against a pillar, briefly considering using an emergency transportation spell, but after a second's thought abandoned the idea. Transportation spells only work if you know where you're going, and I hadn't a clue. Buster was already a small dot in the distance. There was nothing for it but to pick up my skirt and follow.

I won't dwell on the next bit. Just thinking about it gives me a stitch. Imagine a series of bogs, woods, stiles and ploughed fields, with a soundtrack of pounding feet and gasping breath, and you'll get the picture. Instead, let's move on to the caravan.

It stood on a piece of scrubby land surrounded by brambles. It was small, shabby and sagged in the middle. Lace curtains hung in the tiny windows. One or two chickens pecked in the dirt. Apart from them, and the donkey tied to a nearby tree, there was no sign of life.

Buster was already barking noisily at the foot of the rickety steps which led up to the tiny front door. As I came staggering from the thicket, mud-splashed and scratched, the top half of the door flew open and a familiar face looked out.

"Buster? What are you doing here? I thought I told you to stay – hey, Wilma. What's happenin'?"

I collapsed on a handy stump, clutching my middle and sucking in air. I couldn't speak, I was that done in. Alvis clattered down the steps and came loping over.

"Hey," he said. "Are you OK? Should you lie down or something? Here, let me fan you."

He took the straw hat from my limp hand and wafted it around. Just then, there came another voice.

"What's going on, Alvis? Who's this? No, don't tell me. It's Wilma, isn't it?"

I looked up. Coming down the steps was the girl in the picture. Well, she wasn't exactly a *girl* any more. She looked slightly older than Mother. But it was her all right. The same long brown hair, streaked with grey. And a flowing green dress, very similar to the one she had worn in the picture. There were gold hoops in her ears and a wary smile on her lips.

"Hello, Aunt Maud," I said. "Pleased to meet you."

"Well, well," said Aunt Maud. She placed her hands on either side of my head and studied me intently. "So this is my youngest, cleverest niece. You're just how Alvis described you."

"Am I?"

"Oh yes. He's told me all about you and your sisters and your father and your Uncle Bacchus. I really feel I know you all."

"Really? He didn't say anything about you."

I looked over at Alvis, who was currently being licked to death.

"No. Well, I asked him not to."

"Why?"

"Isn't it obvious? I wanted to know how Mama felt about me. I sent Alvis along to test the waters. To spy, if you like. I've been wanting to come home for a long time, Wilma. But I wasn't sure about my reception. Oh, I knew Veronica would welcome me with open arms – but Mama is another matter. I had to know whether she was still angry."

A thought struck me.

"How come Alvis is called Parsley? I thought you ran off with the Sprouts?"

"I did. And very good they were to me, too. But there were fourteen of them, all sharing the one caravan. And they all played tambourines. The noise was terrible. You can have too many Sprouts. In the end, I married a Parsley. He's much quieter. Plays the flute."

"Oh," I said. "I see. Is he . . . er . . .?"

"Still around? Oh yes. He's on tour right now doing the seaside resorts. We'll be joining him. Now that I know there's no hope of a reconciliation."

"Why do you say that?"

"Well, it's true, isn't it? I was so hoping that Mama might have had a change of heart after all this time, but Alvis tells me my picture is turned to the wall." She gave a deep sigh. "Time to move on."

"No," I said. "It isn't. You've got it all wrong. Grandma tried to find you. She told me. She used all her Magical powers, but it was hopeless. You're very good at not being found."

"Well, of course, I had to protect myself," said Aunt

Maud. "Just a little 'Wool Over the Eyes' spell. Basic gypsy Magic. Simple, but effective. But why did she want to find me? Unless it was to bring me back and force me into the Family business?"

"Why do you think? Because she *misses* you, of course. So much so that nobody's allowed to even mention your name. So much so that she can't bring herself to look at your portrait. Why else do you think she shuts herself away in the belfry eating nothing but sprouts?"

"That's right," said a quiet voice from behind. "You tell her, Wilma."

Startled, the two of us whirled around. And Grandma stepped from the bushes. With her was Mother.

"Veronica?" whispered Aunt Maud.

"Maud?" said Mother. To my amazement, there were tears in her eyes.

"Mama?" croaked Aunt Maud.

"Oh, Maud! My Maudie!"

And then the three of them ran to each other, arms outstretched. It would have been better in slow motion, but it was still pretty good. They met and embraced in a tight, sobbing huddle, while Alvis and I looked on, feeling slightly embarrassed.

"Let's leave 'em for a bit, shall we?" said Alvis.

"Good idea, cousin," I agreed. "Any chance of a cuppa? I'm parched after all that running."

"You're on," said Alvis.

And we went into the caravan and had a celebratory cup of tea.

# POSTSCRIPT

There's not much more to tell, really. Aunt Maud's given up the caravan for the time being and has moved in with us. She, Mother and Grandma spend all their time chatting. Well, they've got a lot of catching up to do. In a spirit of goodwill, I offered to do The Round for Mother for a couple of nights, but she declined. I can't say I'm sorry. I like my bed too much. I don't know what kind of Queen I want to be when I come of age, but it certainly won't involve night-time flying.

Grandma's a changed person now Aunt Maud's shown up. The long sulk is over. She's stopped eating sprouts. She's thinking of moving out of the belfry and back into the main house. That's all right, as long as it's not into my room. We're all looking forward to meeting Alvis's dad. He's cutting the tour short and coming to the big Welcome Home party we're throwing in Aunt Maud's honour tonight. I wonder if he'll have the same strange hair as Alvis? I hope so.

I was a tiny bit cross with Alvis to begin with. He could have told me he was my cousin and saved all that trouble. But, as he explained, he had promised his mum to keep his lips firmly buttoned – and I was rather tied up with my own affairs at the time. I've forgiven him anyway. Well, I have to. He's promised to teach me how to play guitar.

Both my sisters are coming to the party tonight. I don't care. For once, I don't think they'll be the centre of attention. Word has got round that I was the one who finally tracked down Aunt Maud and, for once, *I'm* the blue-eyed girl. I've even got a new dress. It's blue. I like it. It fits. I might even try to do something about my hair.

I've still got a few loose ends to tie up. Both Snow White and Gerda have written me nice little thank-you letters, which I haven't replied to yet. One chore I *don't* have to do is let Ogggg out of the Magic Mirror. According to Mother, Scarlettine smashed it in a fit of pique. When I get time – and when Mother returns my Magical equipment – I'm going to check him out in my Crystal Ball and see what he's getting up to. You never know – he might come in useful one of these days.

So. Everything's worked out just fine. I've got a whole new batch of relations, a new dress and a bit of respect for a change. And – most importantly – I've got my revenge.

And is revenge sweet? You bet it is!